RODNEY

Marshall's Shadow Book 4

KATHI S. BARTON

This is a work of fiction. Names, characters, places, and incidents are products of the author's imagination or are used fictitiously and are not to be construed as real. Any resemblance to actual events, locations, organizations, or persons, living or dead, is entirely coincidental.

World Castle Publishing, LLC
Pensacola, Florida
Copyright © Kathi S. Barton 2021
Paperback ISBN: 9781953271952
eBook ISBN: 9781953271969
First Edition World Castle Publishing, LLC,
http://www.worldcastlepublishing.com

Licensing Notes

Cover: Karen Fuller
Editor: Maxine Bringenberg

Chapter 1

Rodney was ready to close up the office for the day when a little boy came in with blood all over his face and hands. Calmly, so as not to freak him out any more than he seemed to be already, he asked him if it was his blood or someone else's.

"Mine. Most of it anyhow. I was wondering if you could maybe fix me up before my aunt wakes up. She's going to have a cow when she figures this out. Man, is she going to brain me." Rodney took him into the exam room and asked him if he could call his mom. "Yeah, call her. That's a good idea. Mom won't freak out until after I'm fixed up. I fell out of the tree and hit my head too."

After cleaning most of the blood off the kid, he could see that he was going to need some stitches. Also, his head was going to need to be X-rayed.

Aaron, he told him his name was, said he'd been in the tree hiding from a bully at school. His sister Angie, he said, had run home when he distracted the bully.

"All right. We'll need someone here that can okay you getting sewn up. Tell me your mom's name." He did. Sheila Walsh was working, but she'd come home for him. "I would imagine she would. And this aunt of yours—I don't suppose you can tell me why she's sleeping when you're out with bullies? You don't have to, but you do seem to be afraid of her."

"Nah, I'm not afraid of her. But she told me she's so stressed out that if she was to fart, she'd have a heart attack. She quit her job. We really need the money, Mom said, but we need Rebel more. She's my best friend. When she's not freaking out." He heard the door open and his nurse talking to someone. When she laughed, Rodney relaxed a little. "Oh no. That's my aunt. Tell her I'm not going to die as soon as she comes in here, or she'll have me naked in a minute and her poking and prodding at me."

"Aaron James Walsh, what the hell were you thinking sending your sister home all by herself? I canna believe you would have— What happened to you?" Aaron told his aunt what he'd told Rodney. "Let me have a look at you."

Aaron had been right. She had him stripped of everything but his underwear in seconds. She looked him over, commenting in a language he didn't know about something she'd find. Rodney stood back, waiting for her to notice that he was still in the room.

He knew who she was. The other night he'd spoken to her at the meeting at the school. Rodney had a feeling then that she was his mate but hadn't pursued getting close enough to her to find out because of the things he had going on here and at the school. But with her so near him today, he knew that not only was she his mate, but she was much prettier than he remembered.

"Whatcha doing with that thing?" Rodney noticed that his nurse, Adaline, had brought in a kit to clean up the wounds and stitch them up. Rebel told him what she was going to do with the scissors. "No way are you going to cut my hair away from anything. I've seen you hack at your own hair. You leave my hair alone and let Doc Rodney do the cutting. You'll have me as bald as Grandpa Walsh was before he passed on."

"It'll only be a wee bit." Shaking his head,

Aaron looked at him. So did Rebel. It seemed to occur to her that she was in his offices taking over. "I'm sorry. I kinda get myself in Dutch when I'm worried. He's my nephew."

"I gathered that. I can cut away the hair. In fact, it would be my pleasure." Rebel handed him the pair of shears. "We were about to call his mom. He was telling me that you freak out about blood."

"Nay, not blood on others, but on my family does bother me. Especially this one. He's somewhat of a daredevil at times. You'd not be able to call his mom either. She'd lose her job if she had to leave work." He asked her what she did. "I was an emergency room doctor until last night. I couldn't take it anymore. They don't seem to like foreigners for some reason."

"You're Rebel Walsh." She nodded. "Yes, I've heard that the nurses are giving you grief. Harris, my sister-in-law, is looking into that. There have been complaints from the patients that they're being pitted against you. For some reason, she thinks you're a much better doctor than most of the staff that works there. Are you?"

"I donna know about that. I work hard. It's hard to do when the staff is forever making it difficult for me. They wouldn't believe I was a physician. Or they did but kept telling the patients in my care that I was in over me head and only a nurse. Not that I have anything against being a nurse. But I worked very hard to be a doctor the same as anyone has." He finished up with the hair trimming, then moved back. "I should have sent him someplace to get X-rays. I just wanted him to be better and not bleeding. I should have been careful about watching them."

"I was going to suggest an X-ray. I have the equipment here to do that." Aaron didn't say much, but he did tell them that not only did he have a headache, but his ribs hurt too. "We'll get all that taken care of, young man."

A little girl joined them in the examining room and sat quietly on one of the chairs. When asked if she'd been hurt, she burst into tears. Adaline comforted her while he went down the hall with Aaron to get some pictures of not just his head but his chest and arm too.

"This gonna cost very much, Doc Rodney?" He said he had been on his way home when Aaron came in, so after hours was free. "Oh good. I'll remember that from now on. We don't have a lot of money. Mom doesn't get insurance where she works yet, but Aunt Rebel had some that didn't cover me and Angie. Life sucks, doesn't it?"

"Sometimes." He reached out to Harris and told her what was going on. *I don't know the whole story about what's going on, but if you could check into this little family, I'd appreciate it. They're really down and out, it looks like.*

I have some information on Rebel. Hell of a doctor. She graduated at the top of her class, like number one. She took her exams here to be able to practice right after her brother died, leaving his wife and two children. Rebel came to the States to help her out. I don't know what the issue is at the hospital yet, but I'm working on it. She quit, did you know that? He told her that she'd told him. *Good. Perhaps you can work with her. I don't know. There is some insurance that should have been paid by now, and I'm looking into that as well. It would put them in the black for a long time.*

Aaron has been hurt. I'm still getting details on that. But apparently, they're being bullied. He climbed a tree to give his sister time to get away. She's here too, sobbing in one of my exam rooms. She said she'd heard about the kids being hurt as well. *Why haven't we done anything about it then? I mean, we need to stop this before I have to step in as my cat and take care of it the wrong way.*

Harris was quiet for several seconds before

she spoke again. *Rebel is your mate, isn't she?* He said even if she wasn't, he'd want the kids safe. *How about we do this, then? It's a long shot because I don't know everything yet, but we put them up in one of the houses we own. No rent for the time being, or ever, and hire the mom to work for us. She was a secretary before her husband passed away, and right now, she's barely making enough money to afford food and rent at the same time. Also, it looks like at one time, she was an LPN. Licensed practical nurses are someone you can work with, correct? You take Rebel in as a partner, or whatever you call it, and I'll see about the kids being able to go to the pack school. That would keep them out of harm's way with the bullies until I can figure out what the fuck is going on there.*

And just how do you propose I make that work? In the event that it might have slipped your mind, Rebel is my mate, and I don't want to start this relationship with her being pissed off at me. Harris told him that all of them had pissed off their mates at one time or another. *That doesn't mean I want to go that way first off.*

Invite them over for dinner tonight. He asked her how that was going to work. *Just charm the shit out of her or something. The mother will be home from her job at about six or so. Did I tell you that she's working as a dishwasher at one of the restaurants we own? Anyway, you invite Rebel. I'll take care of the mom. Tell her you were coming over anyway and would like to get to know her better.*

Yeah, that'll work. He said he'd do it. *If this bites me in the ass, I'm going to take it out on Shep.*

Why Shep? I'm the one making you do this? He told her. *Ah, you're so sweet. I didn't know you were that afraid of me. I love you too, Rodney. But get to work. Before I have to go there and do it for you.*

He had no doubt that she would, too. After looking at the X-rays, he took them to the exam room with Aaron. Angie was calmer now and coloring in one of the books he'd purchased for the kids that came in. Rebel wasn't anywhere to be seen, but Angie said that she'd had a phone call and had gone outside. Nodding, he waited for her to return to tell her what he'd found on the X-rays. When Rebel came back inside, she spoke before he could.

"I don't suppose you need an assistant, do you?" He smiled at her. "I need a job. One that I can work in and not be told I'm overqualified or even underqualified for. This shite stinks."

"I was going to ask you if you'd like to work with me. I have the schools and this office. I'm also part of the hospital team when necessary. It would

help me in keeping up with those different things."
She asked him in what capacity she'd be working.
"Doctor. I don't need an assistant, really. Adaline is
working with me. If you know of a nurse or someone
that will be helpful to you, then, by all means, hire
them."

"My sister-in-law is a licensed practical
nurse, but there isn't much in the way of jobs for
her either." This was working out much better than
he thought it would. "I can have her come by, and
you can meet her if you'd like."

"I tell you what. I'm having dinner at my
brother and Harris's house tonight. How about
you join us there? It's nothing fancy. I think we're
having grilled foods. I'm not sure what that means,
but it's always good." She asked him what the catch
was. "Catch? I'm not sure what you mean by that."

"I'm not stupid, you know. And I would
appreciate it if you're going to be treating me that
way if you just keep your mouth shut. In fact, just
shut up." Rodney told her he'd never thought that.
"We'll see. You're something to me. Mate, I'm
thinking. I didn't know what it was until I came
here today. The other day, you didn't say anything
when we touched. You've known for a while."

"I didn't really. I thought as much, but your

scent was covered by all the others in the room. And your touch, really, was very brief." He looked at the X-rays, then back at her. "I don't know what you have against being my mate, but you can already — at least I hope so — tell that I'm not going to pressure you into anything you don't want. It looks like Aaron has two broken ribs, as well as a clean break in his arm. There is a little bruising on his head that is concerning, but nothing I don't think a little rest will take care of. I'd like your permission to give him something for the pain now."

He didn't wait for her to reply. Instead, he stepped out of the room, closed the door, and leaned against the wall for a minute. Rodney felt like he'd been running a marathon. It hadn't been but a couple of minutes, but he was sure he wasn't going to be able to be in the same room with her if she was forever going to be taking shots at him. Standing up, he went to ask Adaline to fix him up a shot for pain for Aaron.

"You all right?" Rodney told her he was fine, just a little overwhelmed. "I know she's your mate. But I'm telling you right now, if she's going to talk to me like she did you, I'm going to take her down a few notches. I'm just putting that out there."

"I'll have a talk with her." Adaline told him

she'd do it if it came down to it. "Just, for me, go easy. I know you will, but I'm working through some shit here, and I don't care for it."

When he had the syringe ready to give to Aaron, he went back into the room. Rebel was missing again, but he didn't ask this time. After giving Aaron the shot, he watched him as he seemed to mellow out and close his eyes. *Well*, he thought, *at least I've made one of the Walsh family happy.*

~*~

Rebel hated herself. She wasn't usually so snappish to people, especially people she didn't know that well. But there was something about his calmness in the face of all this stuff that was going on that irritated her to no end. When she'd come out here for a few seconds of relief from her own mouth, she called and left a message on her sister's phone.

"We've been invited to have dinner with the Marshall family tonight. If we play our cards right, perhaps we can have leftovers." She thought about that and told Sheila she was sorry. "I'm going to go into practice with Rodney Marshall, and I'd like you to give your notice there and be my nurse. We'll work out the rest of the details later."

The Marshalls were very wealthy. She didn't

know how much they were worth, but she was positive it was a great deal more than she and her sister had made in their entire lifetime—probably several hundred lifetimes. Sitting on the little bench right outside the offices, Rebel looked around the little town.

She'd only been in this country for about two years total. Once when her brother had married, she'd stayed for about six months. Then when her brother had died, she'd packed up everything she owned and came here. He'd been living here with their father since the divorce from their mom, whom she'd been living with. It had been several years since she'd seen Thomas since his marriage, and she was heartbroken when she'd come home for his funeral.

"Doctor Walsh, there is a phone call for you." She looked at Adaline and told her she was sorry. "I am too. I was ready to bite your head off for talking to Rodney that way, but he told me you were stressed out. It's been hard on him, trying to make all this work on his own. He loves it, don't get me wrong, but the schools are in worse shape than anyone wanted to believe."

"I've been volunteering there one day a week, and I canna believe no one has done anything before now." She followed the older woman into the building and picked up the phone. It was her sister. She was crying and screaming at someone else, and Rebel waited on her. "Can you see what I need for Sheila Walsh to be able to come here as my nurse?"

"Rebel? Where are the kids?" She told her what had happened and that she was at the doctor with them. "I came home to find someone here shutting off our power and no kids. I was worried more than I could—"

She was cut off. More than likely, the power had been cut. They'd been expecting it for several days now, and apparently, their time had been up. Putting the phone back in the cradle, Rebel wanted to find a nice dark room and sob. Things couldn't get any worse, she told herself, then amended that to say it could and more than likely would. While she was standing there, Rodney came out of the exam room and asked her if she was all right.

"Not particularly, no." She told him, starting with the power being cut off, what she'd been dealing with in the last twenty-four hours. "The water is next. Though I have explained to the company that we haven't gotten a bill so I donna know what to pay on it. Not that we have the cash for that either. Angie needs money for a class trip.

Aaron is hurt. His mom is at her wit's end, and I'm right there along with her. I haven't any income, and the fucking insurance company won't get off their collective arse and pay up on the insurance that Thomas had when he died suddenly at home. Not suddenly, but he did die, and they should have to help out his family when he made the payments every frigging month."

"Come with me."

She didn't have much in the way of a choice when Rodney took her hand into his and dragged her down the hall to another exam room. There he pulled her into his arms and held her. Nothing sexual about it, but it felt wonderful to have a pair of very strong arms holding her. Even if it was only for a little while.

"Harris is looking into the insurance money for you. When she did a search on the two of you, she said it came up." Rebel looked at him. "She did this before today, and if I know her, she's going to have answers for you by the time we have dinner there tonight. Now. There is something you can do for me that will help you in ways you can't imagine. As a family, we own several homes. One of them is being cleaned up and filled out for you right now. I've spoken to the others, and they're going to move you and your little family into it today. In fact, Shep and two of my other brothers are at your home right now with your sister-in-law, Sheila. I have a home as well. If you'd like to move in there, for the time being, I'll move in with one of my brothers so you can have the entire house to yourself."

"The landlord is a creep." Rodney asked her what he'd done. "Nothing much other than he just comes into the house when he wants, using his own key. If we were to change the locks, he said he'd sue us. That as our landlord, he has the right to come and go as he pleases. Twice now, he's been in my room when I've been sleeping, Aaron told me. I've not an idea what else he's been up to when we're asleep or not around."

"I'll take care of him." She told him not to kill him. "I'm not making any promises on that score. However, if you'd like to go home and help out with the moving, that would be all right with me. The kids can stay here until I go to see my brother. Aaron is resting now, the best thing for him, and I've put a cast on his arm. Angie is taking a nap. She said she did it after school every day."

"You're serious." Rodney pointed out that he wasn't very good at jokes, and he was rarely, if ever, not serious. "What am I going—?"

"Don't. Don't ask me what the catch is. Or how much I'm going to take from you for this. There is no catch. I promise you that I have nothing untoward in my head about you having a place to stay that is safe, as well as something you can afford." He grinned at her. "Your family is now my family, and I need to do this for them. To make you happy. I swear to you on my mom's heart that I'd never ask you or trick you into anything you don't want to do."

"I was wrong to say that to you. I'm sorry." He said he was all right with her being upset. Taking it out on him was better than her killing someone. "That was going to be the next thing on my list of things to do today. The landlord again. He's been…. Perhaps I should tell Harris about it. She'd be less prone to kill him."

"Doubtful. She'd just find a way so it would look like an accident." Rebel didn't know if he was serious or not but let it go. "All right. You head back to the house. Shep said that Sheila is helping a great deal, but she's upset. Something about a call from someone. I'm betting insurance company, but I don't know yet."

After handing her his cell phone and telling her to call when they were about done, he said he'd take care of the kids and make sure they were both all right. For some reason, Rebel thought they'd be in better care with him than they would be with anyone else she knew. As she drove back to the home she was sharing with Sheila and the kids, she thought about what it would be like to have someone love her. It had been a while since she'd even dated anyone that she liked. The last relationship she had recently had been with a control freak. Even after that, she scolded herself. Here she was planning a wedding with a man she barely knew.

As soon as she pulled up in front of the house, she knew something had happened, and it wasn't going to bode well for their ex-landlord. Getting out of her car, she made her way past the police cruiser and the large SUV that was parked in the driveway. Mr. Cort was sitting on the ground with his hands behind his back, with one of the police standing over him. The officer tipped his hat at her and said that Harris and the others were inside. She nodded and went into the house, noticing that there was blood on the front stoop as well as the front door. Mr. Cort was screaming at someone, her she thought, about getting off his property and that he was suing her. Oh well, she was no longer worried about him.

"You must be Rebel." She said she was.

"Rodney said you were on your way. That piece of shit out there is lucky that Sheila found him in the house before I did. I would have killed him where he stood."

"You must be Harris." She grinned like it was wonderful that she'd made such an impression. "Rodney said you'd find a way to kill Cort without it looking like anything but an accident."

"I have before. Tell me what is yours in here, and we'll get it on the truck. Wait, the truck isn't back yet. I knew we should have rented a trailer. Oh well. Are we taking your things to the new home or to Rodney's?" She stared at the other woman. "Okay, I'll take that as a new home. Though I can tell you, we'll just be moving you again soon. I'm pushy like that, just in the event you don't know that yet."

"To Rodney's home." Harris stared at her for several minutes before nodding once and told her she was a smart girl. "I don't know about that, but he's promised me I'm not going to be pushed into anything, and I believe him. You? Not so much. But I also know you'll stay out of whatever is going on with us if asked. You will, won't you?"

"To a point, yes." She turned away to go into the next room but stopped just short of being out of her sight. "I don't have to tell you not to hurt him, do I?"

"I have no intentions of hurting anyone. But, as I told him, I'm not going to be pushed into shit I don't want either." She nodded and left her there.

Going into the kitchen where she could hear Sheila, she was nearly taken to the floor when she leapt at her, laughing.

"They came through. Look at this. It's the full amount. Harris said they'd had it ready to go for weeks but were lazy." Sheila whispered in her ear, "I'm not sure, but I think she made them pay me. Oh, Rebel, I can afford to pay our bills now. And with giving my notice, I don't have to fret as much about having to wait for my first check with you. I can still work for you, correct?"

"Yes. I need you there." The check was for ten grand. It wasn't much of a policy, she supposed, but it was enough to get her some cushion in the bank. "What happened with Cort? Did he hurt you?"

"No, that's his blood. He used his key to come into the house, and I'd just gotten this check. Instead of begging him, like I think he wanted me to do, I offered to pay him everything we owed him. He grabbed me and tried to shove me against the wall before I could get away. I hit him and then kicked him in the nuts while he was down. Harris is the one that made him bleed. She's kinda scary, isn't she? But I'm happy now. So we'll have to forget the little shitter and move into a better home."

Harris was making notes when she caught up with her again. She asked her what she was doing, and when she told her, Rebel told her she could add to her list. The house was in poor repair, and the roof leaked like a sieve when it rained.

"I don't think the furnace works either. The air doesn't work at all, even though he told us it did. Also, if you've not made it to the upstairs bathroom, let me warn you now, don't go in. It won't hold your weight. The kids' either, for that matter. I'm terrified that one night the tub is going to come down onto us while the kids are bathing." Harris wrote it down. "Why are you doing this? I mean, we're moving out — thank you for that, by the way — and he can't bother us again."

"He needs to have his ass kicked, is what he needs. These are terrible conditions here, and no one should have to put up with this. Sheila told me he just barges in when he wants to. That's not right either. The fucker is on my shit list, and I'm going to take care of him." Rebel didn't tell her about her waking up with him standing over her. She figured the man wouldn't make it to the hospital if she did. Harris was one intense person. "I hope you don't mind, but I've made sure that there is food and supplies at the new house for your family. I had no idea that things were that bad for you guys. The insurance company is going to have to pay for that. There isn't any reason for them to have held up the check for that long."

"I was going to call them today, but then I had to go and see to my nephew." She asked about the bully. "I don't know a great deal about him as yet, but I will before too long. I think the kids have been keeping things from us because they know how bad things are here. Or how bad they were. I was really worried about what we were going to do when I didn't have any more time coming to me from work."

"I want to talk to you about that as well. Soon. There is no reason for that either. We've had some issues there for a little while, and I've had enough." Rebel asked her if she took on problems like this often. "Yes. We work on things as a family usually, but I've decided I need to step up some work with the hospital. If I have to go there for anything, I want to know I don't have to worry about petty shit going on that will upset me more."

"Good point. I didn't think of it that way." Harris and she went through each of the rooms that were nearly devoid of their things. They'd not just been loaded up, but it looked as if someone was going into the rooms after they left and cleaning up. "When I came here for my brother's funeral, I thought for sure that Sheila was joking about paying nearly nine hundred a month for this place. It's not worth nine hundred dollars to purchase if you ask me. But she was grieving, and I didn't want to upset her any more than she already was. Now, with the things taken out, I can see that it was much worse than I thought. It's small wonder the kids didn't get sick more than they were."

"He'll have to either pay for this place to be brought up to standards or sell it off. I'm hoping he sells. The Marshalls own the houses on either side of this place, and I'd love to be able to tear the three of them down and put in a nice place for kids to go after school." Rebel liked that idea and told Harris so. "Also, you might not realize this yet, but you have the same input that all of us do on things the family does. Any ideas you have or even suggestions will be welcome."

"I'm not ready for that just yet." Harris said she understood, and they finished up the house inspection. "I'm wondering if I should have told Rodney I was having my things brought to his house. He must think I'm off my rocker a little. We had a little spat before I came here. I might have given him the impression I was a bitch."

"I'm sure you are when you need to be. But I've told him already. You'll have to share your blood with us so we can talk to you through a link. Also, in the event that something happens and we need to find you. But that's not anything we have to be in a hurry for now."

Too much, Rebel thought. There was just too much right now.

Harris seemed to understand and changed the subject to something less personal. She told her of the babies coming, as well as a vampire friend of hers that was coming to see Harris to tell her of the vampire line she was a part of. Jason, she told her, had been looking into it for her since he'd tasted her blood.

It was going to be hard to keep up with this family without a notepad. Rebel decided she'd get one when she was out next. It might help her to keep all this stuff straight. Or not. She had no idea right now. But she was thinking it would be fun.

Chapter 2

Lach didn't know why, but she thought there was no room for error with this ghost. When she asked him, for the tenth time, why he'd waited so long to come to her with his problem, the man would only say that things were not all that they seemed. Lach didn't even know his name yet, much less what he was talking about.

"Without something to go on, there isn't any way I can help you, sir." He nodded and moved around the room. Shep had offered her his office to conduct this talk with the dead man. While she knew he was indeed dead, she couldn't tell what had caused it by looking at him. The babies decided they had had enough of her sitting still and started to wiggle around. "I'm going to have to walk a little. Are you going to have a problem with that?"

"Nay, you are having twins." She knew this, but the way his accent came out, she thought perhaps she might well be talking to Rebel's brother. "You are a beautiful woman. I am enjoying talking to you. However, if you could give me a few more minutes, I'll be able to tell you much."

Walking around the room, she noticed some of the touches that Harris had added to this room. There were pictures of men and women dressed in uniforms. A picture of a man she thought she knew but wasn't all that sure. It looked like the new president. With Harris, it wouldn't surprise her if it was him. Right now, she wanted to tell the man when he was ready she'd come back, but he must have worked things out and started talking to her.

"The check from the insurance company, it wasn't enough. It was for one million, not ten thousand." She asked him who he was. "As you might have guessed, I'm Thomas Walsh. Brother to Rebel and late husband to Sheila. I saw my children today. They are very well cared for, don't you think?"

"They are. How did you know about the money?" He told her he'd taken the policy out himself. "I see. I'll tell Harris. She's working with your wife on that. You said that things aren't what they seem. Are you telling me that someone is out to get someone in your family?"

"Aye, that would be the right of it." Thomas grinned at her. "You're smart as well as beautiful, aren't you? I didn't die as they think I did. When I was brought to this point, I knew things I didn't before. I was poisoned. I know you need proof of such a thing, and I have it in my body. However, I'm not sure who the person is that did the deed to me."

"Was it Sheila?" He just glared at her as if the very thought of his wife harming him was too much. "All right. I don't believe it would have been your sister either. She wasn't even in this country when you passed away. Can you tell me what it was that killed you?"

"Poison. But that's not enough. It was arsenic. Fed to me, it was. A little all the time until it was too much for me to bear with me poor body. Do you know the people that were around me then?" She said she didn't have any idea. "'Tis one of them. The people that would be able to come and go as they pleased."

"Other than the landlord, who else would have—?" He turned to look at her, nearly scaring ten years off her life when he walked through her.

"Don't do that. Don't move through me like that again. That was just weird. All right?"

"Yes. I do beg your forgiveness. But the landlord. Did ye know that he was wanting me wife? That's it. It has to be him. Or his missus. Stranger woman than I've ever known, that one. She wanted us, my missus and me, to have a foursome. I've never heard of— Well, I've heard of it, but to be so open about it. I tell you right now, it made me tell them that we was going to call the police on them." She asked him if he had. "Nay. I began to get ill soon after the threat. I've seen him too. Sneaking into my home when the children are abed. What do you suppose he's up to?"

"They've moved to a safer home, did you know that? Also, Cort is in jail. I don't know how long he's going to be there, but with this information, we might be able to make it a good deal longer. What did he do in your home while you've been away?" He looked out the window and didn't answer her for a minute or two. "Rebel is the mate to my brother-in-law. Rodney. She's going to be working with him, and so is your wife, as Rebel's nurse. I think they make a good couple."

"Rebel is the best sister a man could have asked for. When I was ill, she rushed home to be with me. I passed before she could make it. I miss talking to her every day. She is a good doctor too." Lach told him she thought she was nice as well. "He watches them sleep—all of them. I'm fearful for my daughter. He seems to spend the most time by her bed. Aaron, he protects his sister, as he should, but I think Cort has set tyrants upon him to get him out of the picture. He has been hiding a great deal from his mom and aunt, I believe. Especially when he's come up against them when they're out to get his sister."

Things were falling into place, Lach realized. Cort was working things around so he could get to Angie. Standing up, she looked at Thomas and could see that the man was devastated by this. His face was hard, even in death. He worried about his family very much, and she could see what it was costing him not just to come to her but to know he could do no more than that to save them.

"I'll return shortly. If you must fade, please try to come back. I'm going to get Harris to see if she might have questions for you too." He nodded and did fade. For a younger dead man, he seemed to have a great deal of control. "I'm sorry this has happened to you, Thomas. I truly am. But I promise you, we'll do all we can to get this sorted out."

Getting Harris to come to the office was no problem. It was getting Rebel not to join them that caused the issue. In the end, she did tell the woman what was going on and that she would have to be quiet, as excitement and other emotions would drain the dead faster. She also told her she couldn't, under any circumstances, tell him anything unless he asked about it.

"Why?" Lach said she didn't know, but that was a hard and fast rule. "All right then. I'll keep my mouth shut as much as I can. But please, if possible, I'd like to be able to see him, just once more, to tell him how much I miss him."

"He can hear you, Rebel. You could tell him." She nodded, but Lach could tell it was more than just telling him that. "We'll see how much we drain him today. That doesn't mean he won't return, but this might be more than he can handle in one visit. Understand?"

"Aye. Thank ye." Lach had noticed that the more stressed Rebel was, the more her lilt and accent came through. She loved this woman. And to know that she was indeed a part of the family now made it so much better.

Thomas was gone when she arrived in the room. But he came back, making his way to his sister almost as soon as the door was closed behind the three of them. Lach had to admit, she'd only seen this sort of sibling love with the Marshall boys. It was nice to see that there were humans who felt the same way the men did.

Rebel took notes while Harris asked questions. She would give her the answers that Thomas gave her, and it was a good deal more than she thought the man would have had. Some of it, the things he'd found out after his death, would not be things they could use in a court of law, not without evidence. However, Thomas was giving them enough that Harris thought she could have his body exhumed.

"There are three ways we can go with it. Just so you're aware, I'd very much like to go with number one. Just outright kill the fucker." Even Thomas had a burst of laughter with that comment. "The second one is, as I said, exhuming the body. That won't be too difficult. The current administration is very nice to me since I've been helping with small projects. And since I'm with the Feds, I can perhaps find someone I can speak to about it and get it going." She sat there for several minutes. Lach could see that her mind was going a mile a minute. "I keep coming back to number one. However, I know there won't be justice served with that one. All right, number three. This one is a bit trickier. We'd have to catch him getting into the house. Since you've all moved out, I don't know how to pull this off."

"I know." They all looked at Rebel. "I can say I'm going to be staying there for a few days until my new place is ready for me."

"I don't want to use Angie, but how do we make him believe she's still there with you? As Thomas said, he's fixated on her." That was the tricky part. No one wanted to have a child used as bait. "He might think this is his last chance at her and be a little braver. What can we do to make him stupider than he already is?"

It was Thomas who had the answer. He could, he told them, make the man believe what he wanted. It wasn't a trick he had had to use much on his side, but it was a bit of fun for him sometimes. The plan was easy enough, Lach thought, and that was what scared her. It was too pat, too easy for mistakes to happen. But in the end, it was all they had.

The plan was set, but Harris told Rebel she needed to talk it over with Rodney. Lach knew as soon as she said it that it was the wrong thing to say to her. Getting the okay from someone she barely knew wasn't anything that Rebel wanted to do. However, when she stomped out of the room, going to get his permission, she said, Lach followed. There wasn't going to be any way she'd come between the two of them, but she did worry for them.

They were both coming out of the office when the shouting began. It was Rebel doing most of it, but she could see that Rodney wasn't any happier about what was going on than she was. It wasn't until she started to step around them that she realized her mistake. She was much too close to them for them not to notice her there.

They were both angry enough to absorb energy from the others in the room. It was the only thing she could think that was going on. Rebel seemed to glow with the newfound power. Rodney as well, but his was very little compared to what Rebel was getting. If anyone would have asked her, she would have said it wasn't possible for someone to feed off of energy, but it turned out to be true for Rebel and Rodney.

~*~

Rebel had only meant to move Lach out of the way. But when she went flying across the room, Rebel did the only thing she could think of and put out her hands to catch her. In her mind, that made perfect sense. However, she was a good ten feet or so away from the other woman, and she knew she couldn't have caught her even if her life had depended on it. But just as she put out her hands, the motion of Lach coming down to the floor stopped.

She was suspended in the air like a person who had wires attached to her body to hold her. Moving toward her to help her to the floor, she was shoved out of the way by Oakley. Before she could suspect what would happen next, the room tightened so tightly around her that she couldn't breathe for several seconds. Then she noticed that the room was filled with snarling cats with their fur standing on end.

Two of the cats leapt at one another. When she was knocked to the floor in their haste to kill one another, she heard a feral scream from one of them that made the hair on her arms and neck stand up. Getting up while the six cats seemed to be trying their best to tear out each other's throats, Rebel went to the kitchen. She had had enough of this shit.

Handing her a bucket, Molly, their cook, smiled at her as she turned the water to cold, even going so far as to get some ice out of the freezer and pouring it in the bucket Rebel was filling. They could hear the cats in the other room.

The sound of breaking furniture pissed her

off more. When Harris and the others joined her, they started laughing. Pulling the heavy full bucket out of the sink, she carried it to the dining room and tossed the contents on all six of the fighting cats.

They leapt back from the water, snarling at her now when she set the bucket beside her. Crossing her arms over her chest, tapping her foot, she was happy that Lach went to the door and opened it.

"Get out of this house." No one moved when Rebel shouted. "Get the fuck out of this house, and you're not to return until you can act like humans again. The nerve of the six of you, acting like animals. Did it occur to you to ask what was going on before you started—? What the fuck are you still doing in this house? I said to *get out.*"

They moved quickly now, tumbling over each other, still snarling and swiping at each other. When the last one slinked past her, she wanted to kick out at it, but she didn't know who it was. She was going to have to figure that out soon, but not today. They were all on her shit list. When the last one was out, she heard the door slam as she was taking the bucket back to the kitchen. Molly was laughing harder than she thought was warranted, but it was all right.

"They were acting like children." She told the

older lady she'd thought so as well. "Their momma, she would have smacked them all with the broom had she been here. I have no doubt about that."

She said she'd clean up her mess, but Molly told her she had it. It had been worth the little bit of work to see her put them boys in their place. Going into the living room, where the other women were, and sitting on the couch, they acted like nothing had just happened and that they'd been planning this meeting all afternoon.

"I was just telling them the rest of what I was able to get from Thomas. For a recently deceased, he seems to have a handle on his power better than most." Rebel asked if he was still there. "No. I'm sorry. He must rest a little before he can return. He wishes to see you as well. I'll make sure I call you when I need to speak to him again."

"Thank you." She sat back in the chair. "As you might have guessed, I didn't get an answer from the idiot. I haven't any idea why he thought that getting pissy with me would have any other effect on me than what happened. He doesn't own me."

"I doubt if he thought of that as well. And cats are a very jealous lot." Harris stretched out her legs and smiled at her. "I nearly wet my panties when you went to get water. And the fact that you beat me to getting them out of the house is going to be something I'm jealous about for weeks to come. I doubt very much any of them are going to be very happy when they come back in. If I let them."

"I'd not. They're being big babies. It's not like I hurt her when I moved her." She looked at her hands, then at Lach. "I don't have any idea how I was able to do that. I mean, I'm sure it was me, but the thought of what I did scares the crap out of me. Anyone have any idea why that happened?"

"You were feeding from the others." The man appeared in the room with them, and Rebel knew immediately that he was a vampire. Thinking he was the man they'd been waiting on, she waited on him to speak again before she said too much more. "There is a bit of witchcraft coming off you. I'd say that long ago, more than likely from the Salem witch hunts, one of your ancestors was a strong witch. You could, perhaps, use some of the other magic you have and get stronger with it. However, today we're here for me to tell my friend Harris what I have found out about her. Are we having the men come in to hear this as well?"

"No." They answered him in unison, and Jason laughed. Then Bella explained what had happened. "So we sent them outside, where they might have to live for a while if they don't straighten up their shit. Christ, you should have seen them, Jason. They were like wild animals simply because Rebel got a little overzealous with moving Lach out of the way."

They were laughing when Harris went to the door. Going out onto the deck, Rebel wondered what she was telling them. Hearing Harris getting a little loud, Rebel laughed. Whatever was going on, it was enough to piss Harris off again. When she came into the room again, she smiled at them all and began telling them about why Jason was there.

"Shep felt it might be good for us to know, in the event one of our children was born with the traits of whoever it was. It's nothing I've been concerned about but for that reason." The door opened, and the men came in, Shep leading the way. "Are you planning on starting a ruckus again?"

"No." They came in and sat down on the other chairs in the room. Oakley looked at her, as did the others. "I'm sorry that things got out of hand earlier."

"I didn't hurt her. I wouldn't have hurt anyone in this room unless they provoked me. As the six of you did." Rodney came and sat on the floor in front of her. While he didn't touch her, he was close enough that she could see he was having a hard time keeping his humor under control. "What do you think is so funny?"

"You. Christ. You looked amazing when you dumped that water on us. I wanted to be pissed off, but I just couldn't. Every time I think of you standing there giving us a piece of your mind with that bucket in your hand, I'm going to laugh my ass off. It was amazing." She grinned with him but was still stern when she told him she'd been pissed. "Oh, I don't think any of us thought you weren't. And with good reason too. We overreacted. Or worse, I guess, we didn't think about what was going on before we acted. I will next time. I think we all will."

"Rodney is right. We should have let you handle what was going on in the first place. If you'd like to tell us the plan again, we'll listen. Offer our opinions too." She nodded at Shep but told him she was used to making decisions on her own. "Yes. As have all of us. We, as cats, should have been more supportive than jumping in where we weren't needed."

"I think we should allow Jason to tell us what he knows about Harris. Then, he mentioned that I might have some witchcraft in my blood. That was why I was able to catch and hold Lach. On my own." They dropped their heads again and nodded. "Go ahead, Jason. Tell us what you've been able to find out."

"Of course." Jason sat down and turned to Harris. "Shep was right in thinking you were vampire. Also, believe it or not, there is fae in your bloodline. Not enough for me to have tasted it, but when I did a search on your line, I found, more generations back than I could have found on my own, that you did indeed have a mated vampire and fae as ancestors."

"So he was almost right on both. If you say it's a small amount, then how was he able to taste it?" Harris held onto Shep's hand as she asked Jason. "Please, tell me what you've found out."

"His name was Alexander. If he had a last name, like most of us, it has long since been forgotten. I'm sorry to tell you, however, that he has died. When his mate, Maybell, was killed, he followed her in death by meeting the sun. Together they had nine children, living a full and relatively happy life. Quite unheard of for a vampire to have so many children. And the fact that only one of them was a female was even more so. They too, sadly, are gone." Rebel asked them what had happened to them. "They weren't immortal—the family, I mean. However, they all had mates and begat more children and even more children beyond them. When they reached the end of their lifetime, they died as a human would."

"But I'm a descendant of them." Jason smiled at her and said she was the last of them. The only living child of the Alexander and Maybell line. "They were the first then. The first of my lineage."

"Yes. And to say that they left you a legacy is understating their lifetime. As you may or may not know, when a vampire is killed or dies, his assets are put into a vault for his descendants. Had you not had me check, his things and those of his family, would have stayed locked up for all time. As it is now, I was able to prove you're a child of his blood, and their assets now come to you." Harris said she didn't need anything. "Perhaps. But to not take it would be akin to not acknowledging your line. It is inevitable that the things stored away for him go to you now. The men in charge of such things have been putting things in your name, as well as exchanging the money for current money at today's market pricing. There is a great deal of it, Harris. More than you have currently."

"Christ." Rebel had an idea that Harris was

wealthy. But whatever it was, Shep seemed to be a little upset with whatever was coming to her. He spoke before she could ask him what was pissing him off. "I'm just getting used to having an endless supply of ready cash. You're making it sound as if what we have isn't even a drop in the bucket."

"If the money you had right now were enough to fill one of the oceans in this land, the amount for you from your descendants would fill *all* the oceans and flood the world." Jason paused to let that sink in before he spoke again. "There isn't a number they can give you that will tell you what you now have."

"Can I at least assume it's not all money?" Jason told Harris it was also gemstones, like diamonds and emeralds, property, homes, as well as stocks. "Why hasn't anyone before now at least gotten some of this? I mean, it could have meant a home for them. College or whatever."

"They have. All of the generations got some of it. However, like their sire before them, they added to the vault. There are other things I need to discuss with you if—"

"Who wants something to eat?" No one said a word when Harris suddenly stood up and asked who was hungry. "Well, I am. I'm going to the kitchen. I need a minute. Or a year. Just let me think about this."

No one moved to follow her. Rebel thought about it, going after the woman to ask her if this was something she had planned. A joke or something. But she also didn't know if she wanted to hear that it was true. That the couple whose home they were in was worth billions, even trillions, of dollars seemed too real to be a joke.

"Anyone need any money?" It was Rodney who laughed at Shep first. Then he was followed by Trenton and the others. Lach looked like she'd been hit with something, and even Bella looked a little shell-shocked. "I'm thinking we can pretty much lend any amount you might need for any project you have going or are even thinking about starting. This is much more than I imagined it would be when I asked Harris to call one of her vampire friends."

"I'm not sure you should even begin to put it in a bank. Or several of them, for that matter. This would have people crawling out of the woodwork." Shep told her he'd be able to afford them. "Yes, but it would be something that would get someone hurt. Your children kidnapped too."

"I'm worried about that now. So you're right. We'll have to figure out how to use this money without causing trouble. I'm thinking the first thing we should do is get a vault of our own." Jason said it had arrived in a vault. "Good that— Did you say that it arrived in one? Not that it's coming here in one?"

"It's here in your lower levels. As you could imagine, they wouldn't want to have to care for that much if they had someone around that could take it off their hands. The vaults—plural, so you are aware—arrived just as I did. If you'd like, I can show them to you now." No one moved. "Or not. It's up to you. The passwords are on the front of each of them. Once you have opened them, I'd remove the passwords and change them to something you can remember. I have also left a list of things for Harris to try out. Some magic that she may or may not have already. I can come back at any time to answer questions. We have an established link, so we can talk that way as well."

Jason stood up. So did the rest of them.

"You don't have to leave. She'll be all right, I'm sure of it." Jason said he'd been up much too long as it was. Shep shook his hand. "Thank you, Jason. I don't know how we're going to handle this, but we really do appreciate you figuring it out for us. At least we know a great deal more than we did before with this."

"As is always a good thing. I was going to go and see your grandfather later tonight. The two of us have been hanging out, sorting through photos and things that his wife had made. The two of us, we get to be like sad old men together, remembering Jill Ann and his wife as well." Jason smiled. "I would never hurt the older man, but I must say, he is in a better place than I knew him to be even a few months ago."

"Harris." Jason nodded. "She loves him as much as we do. I believe all the family does. He certainly loves Dru."

"As do I. The young, they can bring out the best in a person. Most of the time anyway."

After telling them goodbye, Jason disappeared. Rebel had a moment to wonder if he could tell her much more about the witch she might have come from, but she'd save that for later. She didn't have any idea what was in the home she was going to be staying in, and then there was the trap to catch Cort. That, she thought, would be a wonderful thing for her.

Chapter 3

Rodney waited in the lobby for Rebel to be looked over. The emergency room had been expecting her to come in, and they'd taken her right back to the cubical she was in. Nothing much had happened to her. However, she'd been covered in blood from her head to her feet. He wasn't sure how he was feeling about that, but he did sit out in the lobby where he was told to sit. Messing up now would cost them a great deal more time than they'd already invested in this guy being out of their lives.

"Are you all right, son?" He nodded, then shook his head at his grandda when he sat down beside him. "Yeah, I have to tell you, I feel the same way. I wanted to go back there with her, but Harris told me they had to do this by the books, or a lot of people were going to be upset with them. I don't know that I care about other people so much as I do that little girl in that room back there."

"I know. But she's right. The law is the law, and if we start making it look like we're above it, there is no telling what sort of things will begin to happen to us." He thought about the blood that had been all over the room Cort had been killed in. "If I hadn't been there, Grandda, I don't think I would have believed it from someone telling me about it. Even with Shep telling me what happened in there, I still have a hard time wrapping my head around it. Do you understand?" Grandda said he did and agreed with him on that.

The night after meeting with Jason, the plan had been set up. Rebel had made a big deal out of going in and out of the house. Even Angie had been a part of the plan. But she was taken out the back, where Cort couldn't see her, and taken home.

Just like he had all along, apparently, Cort let himself into the house, entering the house about an hour after the lights had been turned off. Rodney and Heath had been hiding in the room where Angie was supposed to be sleeping. Shep and Harris, in her official capacity as an agent for the FBI, were in the room Rebel had used as her own when they lived there. Surrounding the house in the back and front were other agents, all of them armed and wearing night vision glasses. It was, he thought, a huge undertaking. Rodney thought at the time that they were making too much of a deal just to make this man pay for his crimes. He would, for the rest of his life, be ever so grateful to his family for treating the night like it was a huge ordeal because it turned out to be just that.

Cort had been released just that afternoon. All they had him on was a smaller charge that would only see him paying a fine and getting to go on doing what he'd been doing. Entering the property without permission wasn't good, but it was a start. Getting him caught at trespassing since Harris had bought the house and land yesterday had him in some major trouble. The man and his wife had been notified that they no longer owned the place, so he had no excuse for entering the home tonight.

The man had entered the room Angie should have been in before going to the one Rebel was in. He didn't reach out to touch the pillows that were made to look like Angie in any way. Nor did he make sure it was her under the blankets. Cort simply pulled out a gun and woke her up by banging it against her head.

"Get up, you bitch. I'm going to take care that

you never fuck with me again." Shep told Rodney he'd wanted to end it right then and there, but Harris had stopped him. Something about he had only pulled a gun and nothing more. "You hear me? I'm going to kill you."

Rebel had sat up on the air mattress she'd been lying on. Shep said there had been a single stream of blood on her forehead, but it stopped almost as soon as he saw it. Like she'd healed that quickly. Laughing hard, she seemed to understand that Cort was going to be ended tonight. But the how of it still boggled all their minds.

"You mean you're not going to poison me, as you did my brother?" Cort laughed like he was surprised anyone had figured it out, Shep told him. "He's told us all about your coming into the house uninvited. Also, we've made sure that your cameras are all turned back on just for this event. You see, we knew you'd be here. And that you'd be trying something nasty with my niece."

Shep told him the man seemed almost giddy knowing someone knew what he'd been up to. Then he went on to tell Rebel he'd been doing this for years, with other renters, as well as other little kids.

"It sickened me, I tell you, Rodney. Made me

want to shift and tear his throat out right there on the spot." Rodney asked Shep what had stopped him. "Your mate. She beat me to it. She beat all of us to killing him."

While he'd not been there when she did indeed kill Cort, he'd heard about it enough times that he could see it all. Not only had Rebel killed Cort with magic that was her own, but she'd done it in a way that no one would question her about being part witch. He was reasonably sure she was as full a witch as he'd ever known.

"Mr. Marshall? Your wife has been cleaned up. She wants you to come back to see her." The nurse looked at his grandda. "If you're her grandda, she wants you there too. I'd be tender with her if I were you. She's having guilt issues right now, and they're overwhelming her. The doctor said she could have something to calm her down, but she wants to see the two of you first."

Grandda pulled out his handkerchief and wiped his face, and then blew his nose. Waiting on him, then asking him if he was all right, Rodney hugged Grandda back tightly, as Grandda told him that he loved him more than anything.

"All you boys and your mates. You've no idea how much you've all come to mean to me. To think I might have missed this without Harris being mean to me that day." He'd heard the story several times in the last few months. How Harris told him if he was sitting by Grandma's grave when she came home, she was going to bury him alive. "I surely am the luckiest man alive, I tell you, son. I don't think there is a man luckier than me right now."

They went back to the room where Rebel was. She was wearing hospital scrubs, and her hair was wrapped up in a towel. He supposed they would have let her shower, but he'd not thought about bringing her anything to wear home. Hugging her, then letting Grandda hug her, it felt like all his worrying just slipped off his shoulders.

"I killed that man." Rodney hugged her tighter when she broke down. "I had no idea he was going to try and kill me until he pulled out that gun. It was like I was doing it all in slow motion. I just thought of him dead and shoved all that... whatever it was at him. I swear there were no fancy moves or anything. I just raised my hands up like a person would do if there was a gun pointed at them. Rodney, he exploded. One second he was standing there with that gun out, and the next, he was just spread out all over the room. Literally."

"Shep said it was you or him. And I'm glad

you were still standing after you took him out." Rodney had never been so happy in all his life as when Shep had come to tell him it was over. "Now that I've had time to think on it, I remember Shep being a little green around his face when he came to get me after it was done."

"Now that I've seen that you're all right, darling, I'm going to go down to the cafeteria and find me a piece of pie. I need it after worrying so much." Grandda asked if they wanted something. He didn't, but Rebel asked him for a large glass of something sweet. "That'll be the magic you used. I'll get you a bunch of them if they don't have anything big enough to fit the bill. I love you, Rebel. I'm so glad you're doing all right now. I'll be back."

When he left them, Rodney pulled Rebel into his arms again. "I was so worried. I knew as soon as Shep came into the room that something had happened. I swear, I didn't even notice the blood on him until I went to the other room. But him telling us not to touch you nearly had me begging to keep you safe."

"I was safe. Even if he'd not pulled the gun on me, I would have been all right. Shep and Harris said they were just set to get him when I reacted." Taking her hands into his when he sat down in the chair, he asked her what made her react the way she had. "I don't know. All I could think about was what he'd said. That he'd been doing what he'd done to our family for years. I have a feeling that once this gets out that he's dead, they'll come forward. It would be shameful, I think, to know he was doing this to me if I was another renter of his. But this will make others brave enough to come tell their story. Cort was a nasty man."

"Harris is looking for past renters. She said his wife isn't cooperating at all, but she's not worried about that. Since the post office is cooperating, they'll find the names of those that used that place as an address." Rodney kissed the back of Rebel's hand. "I've fallen in love with you. I think I have been for some time now, but I feel it now like it's all I have ever felt for you. Will you marry me?"

"Strange timing there, bucko, but yes, I'll marry you. And I've finally given my heart to someone. I thought I'd been in love before. I had, just before meeting you, gotten out of something of a weird relationship. He wanted to control me and who I saw, and I wanted him to kiss his own ass. Neither of us got what we wanted." Rodney burst out laughing. It was a strange proposal. "You laugh, but he seriously wanted me to check in with him whenever I left my job and tell him how many people I saw that day. I thought it was just males at first, but he wanted them all—even the doctors and nurses. By the way, I hated working there. Has Harris had any luck with them bullying other people?"

"As a matter of fact, she said she'd talk to you about it when you're home. Do you get to go home today?" She said they were waiting on blood to come back. "For you or the copious amounts that you had on you?"

"Funny. No, mine. They said that since I passed out—I hadn't any idea that I had—they needed to make sure I was all right. I think I need to get more fluids in me, that's all." Grandda came in with ten bottles of apple juice in a bag. He also had brought Rebel a large hunk of cake, pie, and some fresh veggies for her to eat. She started on the pie after drinking down two of the juices. "I do want to find someone that can tell me about whatever I have in the way of witchcraft. I have a feeling you might know someone, Grandda."

"As a matter of fact, I know a couple of them." The man was forever a surprise to Rodney. He had contacts and information that none of them ever dreamed he'd have. "I'll see what I can dig up for you. The next time Lach talks to your brother, you might have her seeing if he had any of it. With magic as powerful as you have it, I'd say he might well have had a little too."

He'd not thought of that. Thomas having magic. But if he did, Rodney did have to wonder if the kids had any as well. He made himself a note on his phone to talk to Sheila when he got home. Or to have Rebel do it. Things were starting to fall together, he thought. The simple fact that she loved him too made him feel like he could take on the world.

After an hour, not only had she eaten all that Grandda had brought her, but Rebel had also drank down all the juice, as well as three more that the nurse brought into her. When the doctor told her she could go home, they wasted no time in getting her gathered up and into the car. Grandda wanted to stay with them for a few days, and he was glad for it. Rodney was going to the school tomorrow to finish up the exams on the few children that had been out the day he'd been there.

~*~

Harris and Bella were in the conference room when the doctors started to show up. They'd been in there for just over an hour and had the seats organized as to who would sit where. This way, she could get a good accounting of all the people that had shown up. Also, they would both be able to call them by name when they had a question. Harris had plenty of them, as did Bella.

The staff they were talking to today were the ones in charge of different units of the hospital— emergency department head, surgical, as well as nurses—also, the head guy in charge of all the doctors and scheduling. Bella had a list of the names of parents to the children, hospital employees that had roughed up Aaron, and scared Angie as well. They weren't a part of the meeting today, their parents, but they were going to have a long talk with them about how to treat a physician of good standing before she had them fired. No one, not kids or adults, was going to be tolerated in bullying anyone.

As soon as she stood up, Harris addressed the room. "I'm sure most of you know that I'm Harris Marshall. This is Bella Marshall. Mr. Marshall is going to join us shortly. We're part of the board for this hospital. The others, the other four members, have opted not to come today for reasons I wasn't made aware of. However, that won't stop this meeting from being conducted. I would like to address the trouble we've had with one of your doctors. Doctor Rebel Walsh. She has been—"

"We all know who she is." The physicians' department head, James Whit, stood up when he spoke. "We've all heard how she's been making the nurses cater to her every need. That she changes the schedule around to suit herself. We don't need that kind of trouble here, so I'm glad she's been terminated." Bella handed the man a sheet of paper, outlining not only that she'd turned in her resignation but how she'd been complaining to the head of the hospital for several months on how she'd been bullied into quitting. "I don't remember ever seeing this. She must have made this up so she'd look better."

"Have you ever worked with Doctor Walsh?" He said he'd not. "I see. So all this information you have, it's all second hand or more. Is that right?"

"Well, I trust my nurses." Bella asked him why he'd not investigated the trouble. "I have better things to do than to look over every complaint that comes over my desk. Nurse Annabeth Handy would have been able to tell you more than I can."

"Then why are you talking in the first place? I'm sure, like you, that I have better things to do than to listen to someone spout off information about someone that worked for him when he doesn't have one bit of firsthand information about a good doctor." Dr. Whit said again that he trusted his nurses. "I have an application here that I'd like you to hear. Graduated top of their class with a five-point seven GPA. Worked as a surgical doctor not only in their hospital but also was the on-call doctor for all the heads of state for their country. Treated patients not just at the hospital where they did their residency but also worked at the free clinic as a doctor, as well as an emergency surgeon when it was needed. Head of the nursing staff at Mercy General, and worked part-time as a pharmacologist when specialized drugs were needed to combat illnesses that were new to the world. Would you hire this person? Before you answer that, there are seventeen letters of recommendation from not just the other doctors where this person worked but also the nurses. Who, I might add, would clamor to work with this doctor when on shift."

"Right away. That's the kind of physician we need around here. Not one that thinks everything should be handed to them with bells on it." He eyed her before speaking again. "I suppose you're going to tell me that this is Doctor Walsh."

"It is. Doctor Walsh came with a very good

resume, as well as enough recommendations to make me think she should have been taking your place. Since you've made it perfectly clear that you don't investigate problems you might have in your own hospital." He didn't bother answering her but sat down. "Nurse Handy. It's my understanding that you were encouraging the nurses to make sure Doctor Walsh wasn't happy here."

"What a thing to say to me. I have no idea what you're talking about." Instead of calling her a liar, Harris simply turned around and pushed play on the computer she'd had set up beforehand. They all listened to the nurse telling one of her staff members that they didn't like foreigners in their hospital. She didn't like to have them treat anyone that was pure like she and the nurses that she hand picked. She had also made sure that bonuses were handed out to each one of the nurses that could prove they'd made her cry. "Doctors don't cry. That right there should tell you something about her. I did this place a favor by making sure she's gone."

The next program to play had two nurses in a cubical talking to three little boys. They were their mothers. That much was obvious. However, what wasn't clear at first was who they were telling the boys to hurt—Rebel's nephew and niece.

"Oh, don't be such a baby, Wendell. Just knock him around enough that he goes to his aunt about it. Doctor Walsh has got to go, or we'll all suffer. Then when he does, she'll come and talk to me, and I'll make sure you're not in trouble. I want this kid to suffer like we have to when she works here." One of the other kids, his name wasn't mentioned, asked why they had to suffer. "Nurse Handy is coming down hard on all of us because that woman is still working here. Doctor Walsh isn't as bad as Handy says, but I need this job more than I need a good doctor working with me. Just do what I tell you, and things will go better for the three of you."

Harris let it sit there for several seconds before she asked Nurse Handy what she had to say now.

"Nothing. I know what I did. And if any of these doctors were to get up off their asses and look around for a little bit, they'd see that I'm keeping the riff-raff out of their business and running a tight ship here."

"A tight ship that turns away good doctors and nurses." Bella laid a file down in front of each of them at the meeting. "These are the resignations of seventy nurses and other staff members that have been bullied out of a job over the last ten years. Since, you'll notice, Nurse Handy had been in charge of the nursing staff. Attached to each of them are their complaints about being bullied, as well as their resignations. Each of them will have been deemed fired by their paperwork that Nurse Handy has in her office."

"You have no right to be going into my office. The things I have there are private. Not to mention, none of your business. You return all of it right now, and I won't press charges against you." Harris laid her badge on the table, along with her gun and other items that made her able to do anything according to the law. "I don't care what sort of things you say you have. I'll put out a smear campaign that will make you look worse than any criminal you say you've arrested."

The doctors looked at the nurse. Some of them actually moved their chairs back from where she was sitting. Doctor Whit stood up and sat down twice before he finally got his mouth working. He was as appalled as they were at the tactics this woman had used and shocked to the point of not knowing where to start on it.

"Do you have any idea who this is? Not to mention how much money has been donated by her family. We'd not even have this hospital if not for the Marshall family. Which means that you'd be out of a job as well." Bella pointed out that Rebel was related to them by marriage now as well. "Christ. What the hell have you been doing, Ms. Handy? Some of the names on this list were only here for two weeks before they were filing charges against you and your staff of hit men. Yes, that's what I called them, hitmen. They were your little troop of hit men to weed out the staff we thought would make this a better place. When I think of all the doctors that have gone through here, all of them on this list that we were all excited to work with. What would have happened if we'd have put up some kind of fuss? I'm worried to find out."

"She would blackmail them. And if that didn't have the desired effect, she would resort to causing harm to them." Bella had her own information that she'd been working on with her. Lach had also spoken to a few of the nurses that had committed suicide when it got to be too much for them. Bella explained that as well.

Just as she was handing out other paperwork that had come into their hands, Grandda walked in with about a dozen women that had been hurt while working here. Not just mentally by Nurse Handy and her aptly named crew, but also physically. Being on the list of this woman meant you quit or you were hurt badly.

"I'm sure all of you know Mr. Marshall," Harris continued. "With him today are past employees of this establishment. There are a great many more of them, but these people could travel here today. These women are no longer in the medical field, thanks to the treatment they received here. It proved too much for them to have been harassed by this woman. Not just at work, but she also caused them a great deal of issues at their homes. Husbands left them. Wives were told about nonexistent affairs."

"My God. What have you done to us? Do you have any idea what this is going to cost us? Not just monetarily, but with our reputation as a good hospital?" Doctor Whit looked around the room, shaking his head. "I had no idea. You were right, Mrs. Marshall. I've been a lazy doctor if this has been going on under my nose. You'll have my resignation by the end of the day."

"I'm not asking for you to quit, Doctor, but to know that you're coming up on some serious lawsuits that will be won by them. These women alone will drain the hospital of all the profits that have come to this place in the last several years. And they deserve it. What I want you to do is to make sure this doesn't happen any longer." He promised her it would not. "I'm glad to hear that. These women are good nurses and will, with one condition, come back here to work."

"Let me guess. They want me fired. Well, it's not going to happen. I've been here for nearly thirty years. Well before any of you should have been sticky on a sheet. I'm in charge of this place, and it wouldn't be where it is today without me. Firing me would be monumental to closing this place down, and then what will all you whiney asses do for help? You'll not be able to run this place without me." All six of the other department heads stood up. When they looked at Handy, Harris was sure they were going to tell her they did need her. Harris was going to kick their asses if they even tried that shit. "You all should be giving me a raise. Do you have any idea how much work it takes to make sure we have only one race here? As well as no foreigners? A great deal, let me tell you. This worked for us once when they weren't even allowed around white people. It'll work again, but only if you get your head out of your asses and let me do what I do best. Christ, you'd think I was breaking all kinds of laws here. I'm only bending the ones that matter."

"Mrs. Marshall, if you'd be so kind as to call the police—or if you can, arrest this woman—I'd greatly appreciate it. Not only has she admitted to being a bully, but she's been promoting biases against people of different cultures and races as well. I, for one, would like.... No, scratch that. I would love to see her out of here as soon as possible." Harris thanked Doctor Whit and went to the door that closed off the other part of this large office. Her men were there, recording the events of the meeting, as well as standing ready to arrest whomever she told them to. "Thank you."

As they were dragging Handy out, she was calling the men taking her out every racial and religious slur, as well as a few that Harris was sure she was making up. Christ, this had turned out a good deal better than she ever thought it would. Looking at the women that were still there, she started to tell them thanks for coming in as well. But Doctor Whit spoke before she could.

"I would like to offer you all your jobs back. I'm not sure where we'll put you for now, but I assure you that I'm going to be more observant than I was before. As well as taking an interest in the things going on around here." The nurses, all of them, said they'd like that. "If you know anyone else that has been fired or hurt by Handy, I'd appreciate it if you were to ask them to come to see me. Or any other of the men and women here."

That took another three hours. Each of the department heads spoke to each of the women that had come in and not only put them on the shift they wanted but also told them they'd work on other benefits that might be coming to them. They would get paid their full benefits while they'd been off, including seniority and any vacation pay they might have had coming.

Bella and Grandda had gone to get drinks while she ran quick security checks on the people that were there. By the time they were finished up, the hospital had a good staff coming in now, as well as three nurses that were going to work on getting the nursing department overhauled. Which meant that by the end of the day, more would be terminated for their parts played in this entire mess.

Reaching out to Rebel, she was asked if she could talk to her later, as she was in the insurance office with Sheila. Harris had forgotten they were headed there today and told her good luck. It sounded to her like it wasn't going well, and she might just run over there when she was finished here. It couldn't hurt. Or better yet, she'd have their attorney go. Ricky was just saying how he needed to get out more.

Calling him was no problem. He said he'd be there in less than ten minutes, and he'd only sit back and let Rebel handle it unless she asked. He'd heard about the incident with Cort, and everyone was a little afraid of the other woman. Not her. Harris loved that she could get all witchy when necessary.

But almost as soon as he got there, he called her back. "They're arresting Sheila and Rebel. Neither of them are fighting the police, who, I might add, are just as confused as I am. But you should meet them at the jail. Also, you should go and pick up Lach. I think Thomas has been letting the people at the office know he's a mite upset with them." It was humorous, whatever was going on if Ricky's voice was any indication. "Oh my, Harris, this is more fun than it should have been if you ask me."

Taking a few of her men with her, she told them where they were headed. Apparently, they had already heard about what was going on and filled her in on it. Yes, Ricky had been right. It was a good deal funnier than it should have been for an insurance payoff.

Chapter 4

Rodney tried his best not to laugh. It was hurting him in the ribs and his throat to hold onto it, but he figured if he let out another burst of laughter before he got Rebel and her sister home, he'd end up a dead man. But just glancing at them both, as he was also trying not to do, would make him start laughing all over again.

He hadn't any idea what Rebel had in her hair, or for that matter, what was all over her shirt and shoes. But to him, all he could think about was that slimy guy in those *Ghostbuster* movies. She'd been slimed.

Sheila was in worse shape in that she had the sticky substance on the same places as Rebel but was also wearing something that smelled to him like hand sanitizer, as well as some kind of smelly spray stuff. Neither of them were in the best of humor either.

"Did you tell him that you wanted to get the rest of the money?" Grandda didn't even bother trying to hide how funny he thought this was. "I tell you, honey. You look like you've gone a few rounds with some kind of yuck machine, and they didn't turn it off in time. What is that stuff?"

"It's slime from Thomas. If you laugh at me one more time, Grandda, I'm going to make sure you get it on you the next time." Grandda told Rebel she'd not do that. She loved him too much to get him all slimed up. "You have no idea where this shit is right now. I can feel it going up the crack of my ass and oozing its way into my butt. Not to mention my boobs feel like I've bathed them in this shit."

"Now, darlin', I'm sure that's a personal issue there." Rebel growled at Grandda. His calm voice was what was the funniest. "It's a very pretty color, though, don't you think? I mean, they got it all wrong on that movie. Can't think of the name of it right now, but they had it green. The fact that it's all sparkly white makes me think of rainbows and such. I wonder how it tastes. Is it any good?"

"No. No, it's not good. It tastes like slime

mixed with rosemary. I have no idea why that particular herb, but that's what I taste as it slides its way down the back of my throat to my belly. I can't even imagine what it's going to represent when I have to shit this crap out of me."

Rodney laughed. Even had he been able to stop it, he wasn't sure he would have wanted to. He had to pull over to the side of the road and get out. He was hurting so bad from it all. Sure that he broke a couple of ribs while holding it in, he wasn't able to calm himself when Rebel got out of the car with him.

"What the fuck do you find so funny?"

Instead of answering her, he pulled out his phone and let her see the pictures he'd taken while she'd not been looking. Christ, he'd not had this much fun in a very long time. He was glad he'd sent them to a safe place when she began deleting them. He was going to pull them out and look at them when he was having a bad day. He was sure he'd laugh just as hard anytime he got to thinking about them.

"They said they weren't going to have to pay her that money because the check they gave her said paid in full. Did you know that?" He said he'd not heard anything more than that the office had been wrecked. "Yes, well, I might have forgotten how much of a temper Thomas had when he was done wrong. But how he was able to do this is beyond me. I think one of those men in that office has a broken arm. I know I was having a hard time just standing up in there with this shit all over everything and anything it could get into."

"Honey, don't. If you talk about the office or what is going to happen when you shit, I'm going to die. Maybe not from not laughing, but you will surely kill me if I laugh anymore." She glared at him. "Come on. You have to think this is funny on some level."

"I think I should murder you in your sleep. Or better yet, I should rub myself all over you and see how you like feeling this way." His cock stretched at the thought of her rubbing any part of her over him. "You've just shown me your cat. I'm assuming he's wanting me as well. I do want you. Very badly. And if we didn't have people in the car with us, I'd take you right here on the side of the road."

"You're hurting me. You know that, don't you?" She smiled then. Not a lot of humor was in her look, but he could tell she was enjoying herself. "All right. I have a plan. We'll take your sister home, then take Grandda and go home. The first one that is naked gets to do whatever the other wants."

"Deal." She opened the car door then closed it. Pulling him to her, she kissed him like he wanted to be kissed. There was so much in the way she moved her body over his that he was sure anyone watching them could tell. "You had better not be called away or any other thing. Do you hear me?"

"Yes, ma'am."

They both got into the car, and he pulled out into traffic. Rodney was glad no one asked him anything. He wasn't sure he could have answered anything important right now. His thoughts were centered on one thing, and that was having Rebel naked under him. But Grandda spoke about what was going on with all the projects he had going on. Mostly to do with the money he had coming from his job.

"I know the family has a lot of projects going on, but I got me an idea that I can hire a crew of workers and do some odd jobs around the town. People like me, up there in years, could use a little extra cash at times. Well, not me, but some of the others I know." Rebel asked him what sort of odd jobs. "I was thinking like mowing a little bit of a lawn. Or picking up something at the grocery store for a shut-in or something like that. I was even thinking that some of us could go over to the nursing home and read a bit to some that can't see much anymore."

The three of them talked about that most of the way back. The drive back to the house was spent talking about the insurance scam too. That's what it was, too. A scam. He was glad Harris was on top of things. Otherwise, the women of his little family would be hurt. Rodney was sure that once she started digging, she'd find this had been done before by the insurance company.

"That wasn't on the check I got from them." He looked in the rearview mirror at Sheila when she spoke. "I took a picture of the check when I got it from them. I've looked everywhere, including the memo part where they told me it was, and there isn't a note there about it being paid in full. I have it right here, and it's not on there."

"You should contact Harris." Something he'd learned today was that Sheila was terrified of Harris and Bella. They'd done nothing to her, but he thought it was more like the fact that they were no-nonsense women and their wealth. Rodney was glad Rebel was encouraging Sheila to talk to them more. "She'll be able to get with the bank about it. I know most banks take pictures of the checks they cash, so I'm betting they have one of yours."

"I'll do it if you're there too." Rebel said she wasn't going to be able to do it today but that Sheila should get on it as soon as possible. "All right. I really could use the money until you get your practice set up. I hadn't realized we owed so much in bills. Then, after getting a small treat for the kids, something I'd do again even if we had only gotten ten dollars, it was gone. That'll be good money for us, and this will make a nice nest egg for the kids when they want to go to college."

So it was settled. Pulling out her cell phone, Sheila called Harris. He could tell she was nervous and stumbled over what she was trying to say, but she finally got it out. Then when she told Harris her bank information, Rodney thought it had gone better than even Rebel had thought it would.

"I have a picture of it now. But I don't think they'll believe me. Especially after today." While he could hear Harris speaking on the other end of the line, he couldn't tell what she was saying. But when Sheila thanked her several times, he knew it had gone well. After closing the connection down, Sheila sounded as happy as he'd ever heard her. "She told me she'd get me the money. No matter what they say. It's good to have someone on your side that will fight for you. Don't you think?"

By the time they were dropping Sheila off at her home, Rodney had taken three more calls. One of them was asking him if he'd come to the school tomorrow morning to greet the dentist he'd set up. The second one was telling him that the building he'd put his practice in had been updated with new signs, as well as three more rooms that were to be added to the rear of the place had been started on. He thought that was exciting.

Taking the third call, he'd been almost afraid to answer it. It was from a number that he didn't know. Answering it with just his last name, he waited while the person on the other end decided to either speak or get off the line. When the male voice asked if he was Rodney, he asked who the person was calling for him.

"We went to college together. Had a couple of classes. Not that we were friends or anything, but we did have the— Sorry. I'm digressing here. I'm looking for a job as a physician. I've just heard there was a shakeup at the hospital where you're from. I applied there before but wasn't...let's just say I wasn't what they were looking for at the time. I was interviewed by a woman by the name of Beth Handy." Rodney glanced at Rebel when the man mentioned Beth. "I'm getting ahead of myself. My name is Howard Benson. I'd very much like to move to your area and raise my family there. I'm sure you're going to have to do a full background check on me. I'd be doing the same thing."

"Doctor Benson, I'm not in charge of the hiring at the hospital." Howard, as he was asked to call him, said he'd been given his number to call. "Can you hang on just a moment? I'm driving. Or better yet, how about I call you back when I get home? That'll be in about ten minutes or so. I should be able to run down what's going on. I'm usually the last to know."

The man laughed. Rodney didn't know why, but he thought that was a good sign. "I'll tell you what, Rodney. If you'd be so kind as to give me your email address, I'll mail you all the things you need to do a background check on me." Rodney gave him his toss-away account email address, the one he used for strangers or just to check prices on things. "All right. I'll look forward to hearing from you. Thanks so much for your time."

After hanging up, Rebel placed a call to Harris to see if she knew what was going on. When she said she'd just put the ad in the paper about hiring new staff, he was surprised. Rebel asked her if she'd given Howard Rodney's number.

"No, I'd not do that to you without telling you first. I'm betting it was someone at the hospital. Though why they'd do that is beyond me. But I can and will do a check on him for us. That way, we can start filling the positions as soon as we can." Rebel asked how many people had quit over the Beth thing. "Six nurses, but I was going to have to fire them anyway. They were part of the trouble your family was having. Five doctors have also been terminated, not by me, but by Whit. He's cleaning house, it looks like. Which is something he should have done a while ago. He's also setting up a whole new set of rules to go by there. I think keeping him on was one of the better calls made with this thing."

"I've never had any trouble with him. The reason for that is I never saw him. He was forever out of his office on one thing or another." Harris said he'd told her that he was going to be working the halls more, as well as being in his office during posted hours. "If he'd done that in the first— No. He'd have not done anything, I don't think, if I had gone to him."

"More than likely not. But he is a man on a mission now. It could be that he gave the man your number in order for you to do just what you did.

Call me. I don't know, but I'm pulling him up as we speak." She went over the things she'd found as they pulled into the driveway. With them sitting in the car, Harris finished up with the background she had found. "Of course, I'll do a deeper look into his life. But as for what I have about him now, he's not perfect, which is something you don't want to find, but he does look like a hell of a doctor."

"He sent me his resume through email. I'll forward it on to you." She said she would use it, but it wasn't necessary. Not for her. "Be that as it may, I'm going to follow the rules as well. Did you have a chance to see if Rebel has her privileges reinstated?"

"Yes. And yes, she can work there as well. I'm to understand, Rebel, that you've allowed students to follow you for college credits?" Rebel said she'd done it, but not in the United States. "I'll look into that as well if you would continue to do that. I know Rodney does it a little as well. There is a huge tax break for allowing students to understudy, or whatever it's called, for the hospital. They're going to need everything they can get at this point."

Taking his phone out of the holder, he entered the house. Grandda gave him a knowing look and said he was going to turn in early. Rebel went to the kitchen, and Rodney went to his office. The sooner he was able to get off the call to Harris, the quicker he could get upstairs and ravage his mate. When Harris told him she had the email, he asked her if there was anything else he could do for her.

"Nothing. But I would like you to consider a couple of things. One of them is for either you or Rebel to take over the school system for their medical needs. Or both. I think the two of you would be a hell of a lot better at it than having several doctors that each go to one specific school. The second thing is, I'd like you to consider being on the school board. That would again be between you and Rebel, but as I said before, you'd be better than the group they have now." He said he'd talk it over with Rebel. "Thanks. I'm headed out of town for a couple of days. Nothing bad, but will you keep an eye on Shep for me? He gets bored too easily, and that gets him into trouble."

"I'll do that."

She thanked him again then hung up. No goodbye. No see you later. When Harris was finished talking to you, bam, she was finished. He sort of liked the way she did it.

Putting his cell on his desk, he went to the staircase. There standing at the top of the stairs, was the most beautiful woman he'd ever seen. And when she smiled at him, she brightened the world around her. Rodney knew he'd never love anyone as much as he did Rebel. And to know she was his, forever, made him feel like he could easily cherish her for the rest of their days.

~*~

Rebel didn't have anything sexy to wear with Rodney. Not that it mattered, she supposed. They'd been having a lot of foreplay fun since a few days ago. Thinking she'd burst if she didn't get him soon, Rebel even gave up on wearing anything at all. Being naked was the best way to go and save on her clothing. She was thrilled that she remembered to send grandda on his way. Otherwise, this would be very awkward.

"I was just thinking about how absolutely lucky I am to have you as a mate." She asked him if it was because she was easy. "I doubt anyone would ever equate being easy to you, love. I was thinking how much you make me feel like a renewed man with every look you give me."

"That was the most perfect thing to say to me." Wrapping her arms around his shoulders when he was on the same level as she was, she kissed him quickly on the mouth. "I took a shower for you. I didn't think you were all that serious about rubbing your body against mine with that crap all over it."

"I'll take you any way I can have you." Lifting her up by cupping her ass, he wrapped her legs around him. "I could take you right here. I mean literally, right here on the landing."

"Go for it. I'm so wet right now I think I could bathe us both in my wetness."

His growl made her pussy even wetter. When he told her to hold onto him, she watched as he tore his clothing off himself. First his shirt, then the sound of his zipper breaking apart had her throwing back her head in anticipation of him taking her.

The wall pressing against her back was cold. However, it was only a fleeting thought as Rodney kissed her, warming her entire body inside and out. Lifting his head from hers, she could see that he had a spot of blood on his mouth. Licking it off, she cried out when whatever power was in that tiny drop raced over her entire body in seconds.

"Do you have any idea how long I've wanted you? Forever, it seems like." He moved his cock to her pussy and touched off a mini, heart-stopping climax. "You're so responsive. It makes me want to make you come a thousand times before I take you."

"Please, Rodney. Make me come. I ache with the need to release."

He moved over her once again, making her pussy wetter than she'd ever been. When he slid into her, his cock filling parts of her that she knew were only for him to touch, she cried out loudly, not just his name but every declaration of love that she could think of.

"Again. I need more."

He fucked her hard. This, she knew, wasn't making love but giving relief. How he hung on until she was able to come four more times was something she loved about this man. Then when he stiffened, his entire body seeming to bow into hers, she cried out when he bit down on her shoulder and filled her with his own release.

"More." Nodding at him, she kissed his face, ears, and whatever else she could touch of his with her mouth. They were moving again, his steps faltering each time he came to another place he could fuck her against. "You're going to kill me. I'm barely hanging on as it is."

"We'll both die very sated people then." The bed was just there when he pressed her against the door he'd entered and closed with his foot. "Please, Rodney, take me to bed."

"Not yet." He took her again, over and over, until she begged him to stop. Her body felt turned inside out. Her fingers hurt from holding onto him so tightly. When he staggered to the bed, holding her up against his body still, she didn't know if she could take much more. But as soon as he rolled to his back, giving her his body beneath her, she rode him slowly, watching his face for anything she could get from him.

While she'd had sex before, men didn't usually let her have the lead. They were selfish, she only just realized, when Rodney didn't move her around, position her in a way that would be good for him. He let her touch him. Massage tight muscles. Even his nipples, as hard as hers were, seemed to be hers to do with as she wanted.

Kissing the tip of his right nipple, Rebel filled her hand with her own. The taste of him was amazing. His body seemed to call to her to touch and taste him wherever she could. His ribs were licked. Shoulders were tasted. Even his mouth, which moved beneath hers when she kissed him, was different than anything she'd tasted before. As she moved her body over his, rocking over him, she found that she loved being in charge of the pace. That watching his face for his emotions was something she found both erotic and calming to her.

"I love the way your breasts move in time

with your rocking over me." He reached up to cup one in his hands and moaned. "They're beautiful. The paleness of them amazes me. I love too that you have thick nipples for me to taste and suckle on."

Lifting the one he'd been teasing up so he could take it into his mouth made her come. When he bit down on her, Rebel cried out. Not with pain, but how much she loved the feeling that came over her when he did it.

When he rolled her to her back, his body taking full possession of hers, she looked up at him and into his golden eyes. Running her finger over his cheeks to his mouth, she told him how much she loved him. How much she was glad he was in her life.

"I love you so much, Rebel." He kissed her then, his body slowly moving in and out of hers. She thought it more devastating to her body, more everything. "I want to see you filled with our child. I want to have as many as you will allow me to have with you."

Telling him that was what she wanted as well seemed to be all he needed to take her. He'd fucked her before, she realized the difference. But now, he was making love to her. Her body, heart, and soul.

Her body was building up for a climax.

However, she wasn't sure she'd be able to survive it. Even her toes were tightly wound, gearing up for what she knew would be epic. When he held her tighter to his body, hitting her in just the spot she needed, Rebel felt as if every single hair on her body stood up. Then it came.

For several seconds she was falling. Not a terrible fall, but one she knew would change her forever. Once she hit the pinnacle, or whatever it was, she bowed up off the bed, holding tightly onto Rodney. Rebel cried out. It was all she could do to give herself the ability to not just breathe again but to kickstart her body into sustaining her life once again. For as much as she loved Rodney, she knew that for seconds there, she'd died. It was then that she realized they were correct in naming a climax a little death. Because she was sure she'd just experienced that very thing.

When she woke up, the room was lit only with the moon shining through the opened curtain. Looking up, she enjoyed seeing the stars through the opening that had been put there and covered in glass. Rodney snuggled against her, and she felt her eyes grow heavy as she listened to his soft snores.

The second time she woke, she was wrapped around Rodney. He was still asleep, but she really needed to get up and go to the bathroom. Sliding out from under him the best she could, Rebel laughed when he pulled her back to him and snuggled up under her chin.

"I have to go to the bathroom, my dear." He groaned but did allow her to get out of the bed. As soon as her feet touched the floor, every muscle she'd stretched out with Rodney made itself known to her. "We need a hot tub if we're going to make love like that again."

"We do have one. But I've not filled it yet." He rolled to his side and looked at her. "I scratched you up a bit too. How about you come back here—?"

"No more sex right now." He pouted at her but did ask her if she wanted to go and get breakfast with him. "Yes. So long as you remember I have an appointment at ten with your grandda's friend. The witch."

"I did forget. All right. We'll do breakfast, then you go to your appointment. After that, we're supposed to meet with the rest of the family for a late lunch. Harris and Shep have figured out the money she inherited, and she wants to talk to us about it." She told him she wasn't family. "Where on earth did you get that idea? You're as much family as I am. Now get your shower before I come in there and scrub your back. If I do, we'll never make anything we have to do today."

Taking a hot shower did loosen her up a bit. By the time she was getting out, she could move much easier and reach for things she wouldn't even want to try before she had her shower. Rodney was on the phone when she entered the bedroom, and since he didn't look upset, she dressed.

She was going to have to get more clothing, she realized. Most of her things consisted of scrubs and tennis shoes. Rebel did wonder if she needed something dressier. The women of this family didn't dress up every day, but when they did, it was in nice slacks, as well as heels. She didn't even remember the last time she'd had on a pair of high heels.

"That was Howard. He said he got an email from Harris this morning and that he was invited to come to an interview tomorrow. I guess she's setting us up to do those for the hospital. Have you ever interviewed a doctor before?" Rebel told him she'd not interviewed anyone before. "Me either, for that matter. I'll have to see if she has some sort of list we can use to go by. You know, questions to ask. Anyway, we're going to be doing those as well as being helpful for the nursing staff. I guess Whit rehired all the ones that had been fired or quit. At least ones that would come back. He seemed really proud of that."

"They should never have been fired in the first place. I hope he knows that." Rodney smacked her on her bare bottom as he went into the bathroom. Posing her question about clothing to him, he said he'd love to see her in heels and nothing else. "You know, that's not the least bit helpful, you moron. I can see the look on your grandfather's face now when I show up in nothing but a pair of red heels."

"Yes, red ones. They'd be beautiful with your hair. But as for Grandda, he'll have to get his own woman." Rebel was glad she loved Rodney, or she might well be tempted to murder him. "By the way, we're going to have to get both of us some more clothing. Not just dressy, but casual as well. I've got a closet full of greens, but nothing much else. The company I rent them from, they wash them and return them, so I never had to do laundry. Now that I would love to go out with you a great deal, I would like something nice. How do you think I'd look in a pair of red heels?"

Yes, she thought, she was going to murder him anyway. As he washed his hair, all sorts of ways to make him suffer came to mind. Walking to the commode, she flushed the toilet and left the room when he started cursing. Smiling, she thought this might be more fun than she'd imagined. Having someone around that was fun.

Going to the kitchen, she was happy to see that someone had made juice. Pulling out the tallest glass in the cabinet, she filled it and sat at the table. After drinking it down, she watched as it filled to the rim again. Not touching the glass or the pitcher she'd pulled from the refrigerator, she decided that if this was her doing, she wasn't sure she was all right with it. But if it was the work of something or someone else, she wasn't all right with it at all.

"Are you all right?" She shook her head, not looking away from the glass. Grandda sat down across from her as she told him what had happened. "You do know it's happened before, correct?"

"I think I would have noticed when— The bottle I took home with me from the hospital. It refilled, didn't it?" He nodded at her as he stood up and began pulling things from the fridge. "We're going out to get breakfast. You're more than welcome to join us."

Putting the things back, Grandda told Rodney what was going on when he entered the room. They both got a little laugh about it, which pissed her off more. But she was afraid right now. Terrified that if she turned her anger on them, she might well hurt one or even both of them. She'd never been so glad for an appointment as she was for the one coming up soon. Perhaps this person would tell her that it was all a joke and that she was as human as the next guy. Somehow, she didn't think that was going to happen any more than her not being able to watch the juice glass fill again. Christ, she was going over the edge here.

Chapter 5

Darin wasn't sure if he was in on some sort of joke or not. The woman sitting across from him, with her head between her knees, was someone he'd not been looking forward to meeting all day. Now, here she was, begging him to tell her it was a joke. Darin no more got that than he did why the woman didn't know she was a witch.

"I didn't know. I promise you, this isn't a joke. I had no idea that anything I was doing wasn't just a fluke." He assured her it wasn't. "Yeah, I got that part. What I don't understand is how you can tell that without touching me hand or something."

Her accent was coming out a bit stronger now. When she'd first sat across from him, he thought she was just like every other want to be he'd ever met. But Rebel was the real deal. Not only that, but her obvious strength was also something she'd never used before. When she sat up, he smiled at her.

"I'd like to just shoot questions at you as they form in my head. Are you all right with that?" Darin said he would do whatever she needed. "Is this because you're going to be helpful, or because of — What is it you called me?"

"Grand witch. And it's a bit of both. While I can see you're really struggling here, a large part of me wants to beg you to let me live too. I know you said you weren't in the mood to kill me right now, but I have to admit, that's not really an answer I wanted to hear." She told him she was sorry about that. She wouldn't kill him. "Thank you. I do appreciate that. You *are* a grand witch. There are a few more around, none of them nearly as powerful as you are. One of them, I'd say, is only a grand because that's what she calls herself. You, you're what we call born to the occupation."

"But I know nothing about this." He said if she'd allow him to do it, he could wake all of the power she had. "Is it dangerous? Not to me, but to you?"

"Dangerous? No, I wouldn't think so. Not unless I offend you in some way and you carry through with your threat. However, helping you would give me a great deal of pleasure. We, people with witchcraft in our blood, have been awaiting someone like you to come along for a very long time." She asked him if he was old. After laughing a little, he realized she was serious again. "Yes. I am. Very old. But because of my magical abilities rather than something like being given immortality. You, however, are immortal. A true one, if I don't miss my bet. And if you have a mate, which I'm assuming you do, then he will be as well. Also, he'll have a bit of your magic. By a bit, I'm thinking he'll be as powerful, if not more so than the leader of the shadow he belongs to. I'm assuming that Grandpa Marshall is related to you in some way."

"My mate's grandfather." She looked around the room the two of them were in. It wasn't a real place, only an illusion he'd manufactured, so she'd not know where he lived if this didn't go well. "We're in the middle of an open field. I didn't see that when I first got here. I did think it strange when a cow walked through here a few minutes into this, but not so much anymore." She looked at him. "Something tells me you're going to be very helpful to me."

"I can. I would love to be your second in this. A person that can lead you, guide you through some of what is going on with you. However, I will tell you again, you only need someone to wake the magic in you, and you'll know and understand everything. Including things that as only a warlock, I won't know." She told him not to do that. "It's up to you, my lady."

"No. I mean saying you're *only* a warlock. You're very powerful in your own right. You also are all white, with an occasional bit of dark when it's necessary. Such as when it's tossed at you." He nodded, telling her that she was right. "I want you to wake this in me. If it happens the way I think it will, I'm sure I'll have more questions than the million and one that are swimming around in my head right now."

Now that she'd okayed him helping her, he wasn't sure he wanted to be responsible for anything that might happen to her when he did this. However, she had told him to wake it, not asked, so Darin had no choice but to do just what she'd told him to do. Reaching out to touch her, he said a small spell that would protect him from whatever happened and touched his fingers to her chest. His entire world just blinked out.

"Wake up, damn it!" Darin looked at Rebel, realizing first of all that she was taller than he'd thought. Then he realized that he was laying on the ground and that he had been out for some time. "Are you going to sit up, or am I going to have to zap you again? You scared the living shit out of me. Why didn't you tell me it would hurt you?"

"I didn't think it would. I put a protection spell around me." She asked him how he thought that worked for him. "You're very snarky, aren't you? I'm fine. Just a little off balance."

Sitting up slowly, he did feel slightly off balance. Sitting there with his eyes closed, he took a quick inventory of his body. Nothing was broken or harmed, but he was a little more powerful than he'd been when he'd agreed to meet her here.

"You gave me a bit of your magic." She said she'd zapped him. Darin looked at her. "I'm not at all sure what that means. You zapped me, how?"

"When you flipped backwards out of the chair, I had to revive you. You were dead when I touched my fingers to your pulse. I just thought of shocking you a little to get your heart beating again, and it worked. Don't do that again. You hear me?" He nodded at her as he stood up, feeling better by the moment, his mind still stuck on the fact that he'd been dead. "I know a great deal now. It's not as overwhelming as I thought it might be. I also know enough to tell you that you're not magically immortal anymore. You're as true to it as I am. I guess zapping you gave you that."

Sitting down, hard enough to make his teeth snap together, he looked at the young witch. A great many things were going through his own head right now, and none of it was about teaching this woman about her newfound powers. She'd saved his life.

"Do you know that had you let me stay dead, you'd have gotten my magic as well as whatever came to you by your birthright, don't you?" She said she did but didn't want him dead. "For what reason would you not want to kill someone as powerful as I am? You will have to do that someday, my lady. There will be others that come for you, trying very hard to take your magic and powers from you."

"For now, I'm not going to worry about that. I'm sure that when the time comes, I will not only have a better handle on things but what most don't know is that I have my own familiar in the form of a very powerful jaguar. That will not only make me more powerful, which I don't know how the hell that's supposed to work, but with him at my side, I'm pretty much invincible." Darin was beginning to really like this woman. She was far from what he thought she'd be when he'd been first approached by his good friend Grandda Marshall. "I do have a question I'd like for you to answer if you can. You'll notice I'm careful not to demand anything of you. I wish I had known that before, but now that I do, I'm not going to treat you as a servant of mine, but my friend. The question. All right. What can you tell me that would involve me challenging the lesser witch that claims to be a grand witch? She's causing trouble for our kind, and she needs to be either ended or made to see the error of her ways. Before someone else gets hurt, I mean."

"You can feel all the witches and warlocks around you, correct?" Rebel nodded. "Good. That was something I learned from your zap, that you're much more powerful than even I first thought. But to challenge her, you need only to tell her to step down or face the consequences of your wrath. You must tell her, in your own way, that you're not happy with her current way of doing things. As her superior, you must tell her from the start that you're stronger than her and know that you'll be required to take her to task."

"So in other words, I tell her to stop fucking around, or I'll have to fuck her up. That's it?" Darin laughed. Hard and long. She was like a breath of fresh air in his world. When he nodded, telling her that was it precisely, Rebel grinned back at him. "I'm really good at telling people like it is rather than beating around the bush to get back where we started in the first place. With this magic, I can summon her here, or I can go to where she is. How does it work if…? Never mind. I got it. Hang onto your hat, Darin. We're going for a ride."

He found himself standing in a large room with not just Wendy, the witch, but several other lesser witches, as well as wannabes. When the ones that were down on their knees, seemingly bowing to Wendy, saw them, they all fell to the floor on their bellies as soon as Rebel cleared her throat.

"What the fuck are you doing?" Wendy tossed a spell at Rebel when she spoke. However, the effect it had on the stronger woman was that she absorbed it rather than it hurting her as Wendy appeared to have wanted. "Stand down, or so help me whatever you threw at me will be a walk in the park compared to what I will do to you."

Rebel looked at the ones on the floor and told them to be gone. Darin figured they'd leave on their own, but they simply disappeared. He didn't ask her what she'd done with them but waited until this was finished before he started questioning her methods. Telling Wendy to sit down had the witch not just sitting on the floor, but her hands were bound together with magic, and her mouth seemed to be glued shut.

"Now, here is what I'm going to tell you. Only this one time so that you can ask me questions if you wish. But I'm telling you right now, you fuck with me, and I'm going to kill you. It won't be a pleasant send-off, either. I will make you suffer in ways that what you've done to your victims looks like a day at the zoo. Nod if you understand me." Wendy screamed behind her closed mouth, and that was when Rebel simply snapped her fingers. "You may speak, but I want to warn you once again, I'm not one to fuck with."

"Who the hell do you think you are coming in here like you own this place?" Rebel said she was sorry and told her what her name was. Also, he was glad to hear her declare herself as the grand witch. It would be her saving grace to tell anyone that asked about today that she had warned the other woman. In introducing him, he was glad to hear only their first names when she finished speaking. "I don't give a shit what your name is. What do you hope to gain by pissing me off? I will tell you right now, I'm going to put you into a world of hurt myself when I'm free from this magic."

"I want you to think about what it is you're saying. Not only was I powerful enough to send your would-be victims away, but I was able to order you to sit and bound you in a way that prevents you from using your…well, your paltry magic. Do you know that only someone more powerful than you could have done that?" Wendy stupidly said Rebel wasn't more powerful than she was. "Okay, let's test that theory of yours. I'll allow you to try and harm me once. If that doesn't work, then you'll concede to the fact that I'm not only stronger than you are but apparently a good deal smarter than you are too."

As soon as she was freed from the magic, Wendy stood up and gathered strength around her. The magic was dark. He was able to see that now, and when she shoved it at them, not only was he not hurt by it, but neither was Rebel. Again, she seemed to take it as her own.

"Is that all you have?" Wendy screamed out her frustrations and tried again. This time it was powerful, but nothing that harmed either of them. "I can see that you're wearing yourself out. Would you like a few minutes to recoup before I shove it all back at you? I have to tell you, I had hoped this would go better than I thought it would. You've broken a hefty rule. One that, even as a lesser witch like you are, will get you into serious hot water with the other witches."

"If you leave right now, I won't report you to the council." Rebel said they were there, and as if they'd been summoned to show themselves, the nine witches of the board showed themselves. Wendy turned to them. "She came here to kill me. Not only that, but she disbanded my helpers."

"We've seen enough, young Wendy. You have been a blot on our kind for many years. Even as a novice, you were showing others what you could do when there was no reason for it. You've caused harm to those lesser than you, even going so far as to kill humans that had no more power than a newborn cat might. No, you've taken this too far this time, and we're happy to have one as strong as Rebel Marshall to call you on the carpet."

"You can't be serious." The witches nodded as one. Darin hadn't called them there, but he was ever so glad they were. Whatever was going on, it wasn't going to end well for Wendy. He had a feeling that she'd either be dead by the end of this or so broken she might wish for her death. When the council looked at him, he felt his own cock, long since lying dormant, tuck itself closer to his body.

"You are the grand witch's helper?" He started to tell them he was, but Rebel said they were partners. "Warlock, you have attached yourself to a good person. We're quite jealous that you get to be with someone so powerful. Thank you for doing this for us and all witches."

"It's been a pleasure working with her." Rebel winked at him when he spoke. "What are your plans for Wendy? I would like to say that she is redeemable, but she isn't. For a great many years now, she's been like a monster. I only had to mention her to Rebel, and she came right here to make sure no one else was murdered."

"That is why we came. To make sure we took the right course of action. I believe you both will be a good source of help for all of us." The man doing the speaking looked at the others that were with him before turning back to Rebel. "We nine, as a whole, wish to give both of you more magic. It will, we think, make you more powerful than you are now. But it will also keep you safe from others like Wendy here. As to what we will do with her?" Wendy disappeared mid-scream. "She will be taken care of. Thank you."

Rebel turned to him when he felt the magic wash over him. When she steadied him, he didn't complain about it. He was a little dizzy, as well as lightheaded. Closing his eyes when she told him to, they were suddenly in a lovely home sitting in what he thought the heart of the place. A young man, he thought her mate, seemed to be waiting for them.

~*~

Rodney listened to what was going on, also keeping an eye on his mate. She was nearly glowing with magic, and he was ever so proud of her. He had a few, quite a few questions of his own, but he thought they could wait. Rebel was telling him about her meeting with the man that looked as confused as he felt.

"You're not listening to me." Rodney promised her that he was. When she put her hand on his head, things in his mind, questions he'd been dealing with, seemed to have answers all of a sudden. Looking up at Rebel, he asked her what she'd done. "I gave you what Darin did me. An understanding. Also, I guess you could call it, an awakening. Your magic is now as powerful as mine. And yes, your cat is as well. He's bigger too."

Nodding, he looked at Darin. "You've been busy, I guess. I had no idea there were so many witches around. It's like I have a location on all of them. Is that normal?" Darin told him he was feeling them as well, but he did say he doubted anything would be normal about this with the two of them. "Yes, I can see that too. Rebel is good at shaking things up for me. But I love her, and I'd not have it any other way."

"Yes, I can see that you two are matched well." Darin stood up after speaking. "I must be going home now. I have a great deal to do now that I'm stronger. I will need to reinforce things that I took no heed of before. Great power comes with great responsibility. I'm sure you know that, but it is something to think about."

"Yes. I've thought of very little else since this morning. Thank you for your help, Darin. You'll still be my partner in this, correct?" He said he would enjoy that. "Good. I'll call on you when I need you for backup. I'm sure you know I have a bit of a temper, and I might need you to calm me."

"What about me?" He didn't like the way the two of them looked at him. Like they were thinking of where to stick the knife. "I don't think I want to know. Do I?"

"You are my familiar, Rodney. I didn't know that that was an actual thing, but apparently, it is. You will keep me safe and steady. But more importantly, you'll be at my side when I fall apart after passing judgment on someone. And I will do that, a great deal more than I think I want to." Darin said that it would lessen, the stress of it, as witches realized that someone was around to take them to task. "I suppose, but I don't have to like it, do I?"

"I would be terrified if you were to like it."

The man disappeared, and Rebel sat down next to Rodney on the couch. She laid back against his arm that he'd put around her and closed her eyes. He asked her if she was all right.

"I am. Just exhausted. I'll have to have ready juice and sweet stuff around all the time if I'm going to be doing this." She looked at him. "I would very much like to take you out to lunch."

"We're having that thing with my family today. But I'm sure we can work in dinner. If you'd like." Wiggling his brows at her caused her to laugh. The sound of it was wonderful to his ears, and he decided to make sure he made her laugh a great deal more. "Also, while you were out, you got a phone call from the insurance agency that is handling your brother's insurance. They would like you to come in, so this can be settled. I've already told Harris, and she said she'd go with you. Did you know that when you're out and about doing this witchy stuff, I can't contact you? I wonder why that is?"

"You can now. You just had to understand it." He nodded, thinking that while he did have a great deal more information he'd not had before, there was still a great deal he had to learn. "Would you go with me? I have a feeling I'm going to need to be bailed out of jail if this goes wrong again."

"I thought you'd need me. So I had Adeline close up the office today. There weren't any appointments that were emergencies, but she said she'd be there if any came in." He stood up, pulling her from the couch too. "Let's get this done so we can head over to Shep's home. I'll be glad when we have some quiet time for just the two of us."

"I will too, but I'd not expect that anytime too soon." Rodney didn't. That was the thing about having such a powerful person in your life, he'd discovered — there was always something going on that needed attention. "I'm ready. Tell Harris we'll meet her there."

He found himself outside the office of the agency. When Rebel giggled, he pulled her to him and hugged her tightly. This travel thing was nice, but it was a little taxing on the mind. Going into the place, he was surprised to find not just Harris there but also Shep.

"We just showed up here." Shep shook his head

as he continued. "I don't know what happened, but if you two did it, I'd like a little warning next time. What if I had been in the shower or something?"

"I would have known." Would he too? It bore thinking about. Taking Rebel's hand into his, they went to the elevator. "This will go much faster if you don't mind me taking over. I have a way about me that will make sure that a lot of people get their money from these bastards."

They were all in agreement that she could be in charge. Shep said so long as he wasn't covered in that goop from the other day, he was fine about a lot of things. Rebel didn't answer him, and Rodney thought that was funny too. It would do Shep some good to be slimed by a ghost. He needed some loosening up.

The men were all seated and waiting for them, which he thought was particularly strange as they hadn't scheduled a time to be there. As soon as they were seated, the man, Mr. Crumble, started telling them that the check had been cashed and things were out of his hands.

"How many times have you done this before me sister?" Rodney watched the man struggle with answering her. "I'm thinking not only do you have a good accounting of it, but right to the penny on how much you've scammed from them."

"I have no idea what you're talking about." The other man, his name was Saulnier, looked at Crumble. "What is the matter with you? Tell them we're not going to pay them any more money."

"Five hundred and twelve times." It hurt the man to say that, Rodney realized. He was still fighting whatever Rebel was doing to them. "It's been extremely profitable to us, and we're going to keep right on doing it."

Smiling at him, Rebel shook her head. "No. I'm afraid that doesn't work for me. Not to mention all the other people you've taken advantage of. I tell you what you're going to do. I want you to call your offshore accounts manager and have them wire the money directly to Harris Marshall. She'll make sure all the money is returned to the rightful owners." Harris said she could do that. "What are you doing just sitting here? Get up off your asses and do what I told you."

Rodney was impressed. Shep, he thought, was afraid of Rebel and her new magic. But the two men did what she'd told them to do after getting the information from Harris as to where to send the money.

"That's very good of the two of you. Now, I

know that you both have quite a bit of money in your bank. That will need to be given to her as well." Crumble asked what they were supposed to live on. "I don't really give a shit if you live or die right now. Billions of dollars have been taken from good families, and you knew just what you were doing when you did it. Empty your accounts now by writing a check made out to whomever Harris says. Then we'll talk about the little toy collection that you have."

It took them only an hour to get things gathered up before they were finished with the things that needed to be resold—three boats, several cars, as well as ten homes all over the world that they'd purchased with the money that didn't belong to them.

He did worry at one point when the men's noses started to bleed. But as soon as he checked to see if their minds were stressed, he found that they were plotting to not just kill Rebel for what she was making them do but to continue doing what they were doing now. He wasn't going to shed a single tear for them. They'd hurt a great many families depending on the money from the policy their loved one had taken out with their company.

The money totaled more than he thought it

would have. Of course, they'd had to sell the items such as the boat and cars at a loss, simply because they were used. But the homes generated more than had been paid for them, so he thought it was working out better.

"I will need the names and addresses of everyone you scammed. I know you have a list of them someplace. Either hand it over to Harris, or I'm going to take it from you. And let me warn you now, I won't be gentle about getting it." Crumble, even after all she'd made them do, still bulked at the idea of handing over the information. He did it at great cost to himself, and when Saulnier gave Harris the file he had in his desk, the man was sobbing like a baby. He was the weak link in this, he realized. Crumble was the one doing most of the scams. When Harris okayed what she'd been given, she stood up and told them both they were under arrest.

"Wait a damned minute. We both cooperated. We gave you everything you needed. Even things that belonged to us. I'll not have you arrest us too." Harris asked Saulnier why he thought he was above the law. "Because we are really good at this. I mean, sure, it was against the law, but we did give them some of their money. That should count for something."

"It does. I've not shot either of you yet."

Her men came into the room and handcuffed them both. They were still bitching about how they'd helped them when they were taken away. The best afternoon he'd spent, Rodney thought, was getting something to go right for a lot of people.

Rodney had the pleasure of going to the staff and telling them the insurance agency was closed down and that they'd be hearing from the government on whether or not they'd be called in as witnesses. He watched them. Most of them, he thought, weren't surprised by the closure, and one of them did a little dance when he told them that they needed to turn in any keys they had. Harris told him it would have been difficult for them not to have known what was going on in a place this small. It would be more difficult, she thought, for them to be around town.

"People would have known where they worked and spoken to them, figuring they might be able to help them in some way. I've checked, and their employment rate is high. The turnover here is more than most larger companies have." Rodney asked Harris if they could help them in some way. "Yes. I have it on my list of things to discuss with everyone when we get to my house. You're still coming, aren't you? I do have a couple of favors, after seeing Rebel at work, that I think she can help me with at my job. I had no idea she was this powerful, did you?"

"I am as well. She also told me that my cat is bigger than even Shep's. I'm sure I can tell you that whatever you need from us, we'll help you as much as we can. You know that, correct?" She said she did and kissed him on the cheek. "What was that for?"

"For not freaking out. For being my brother-in-law. For the hundred and one things that you do for me every day that I don't know about." She kissed him again, this time hugging him as well. "I just don't know where I'd be right now without all of you around me. Not just in my job, but just about everything. You all have saved my life. I hope you know that."

"I do. But I think you're giving me much more credit than I deserve. I believe it was Grandda that saved you. We just took you into our hearts to love." She started to cry, and he didn't know what to do. Hugging her right now seemed somewhat dangerous with Shep glaring at him. "If you start sobbing, Shep is going to have me for dinner. And I can't go against him, no matter how big I am."

She looked at her mate. "Oh, do behave. I'm telling your brother how much I love him and his wife." Harris hugged Shep, and he calmed down. "All right. Food is on the way to my house for us. Why don't you follow us there, and we'll get this thing started? It's a great deal of money we're going to have to figure out how to spend. And I, for one, would absolutely love to be able to spend it smartly. Or at least have fun with it."

Rebel was napping as they drove to Shep's home. She said she was exhausted, so he stopped on the way over and picked up two gallons of orange juice for her. Knowing that fresh-squeezed was better for her than not, he thought about getting them a juicer so they could make whatever she needed all the time. Smiling as he walked out to his car, he thought this magical crap was beginning to be a lot of fun. Now all he had to do was figure it out. Rodney wondered how much help it would be to their practice too.

Chapter 6

The list that was given to him from the school board looked smaller than he thought it would have been. Heath then realized he'd only been given a part of the needs the school had. His brother Trenton had been given one, as well as the others in the family. They were comparing the lists when Shep stood up and handed them each a credit card. It was from the account now called Special Projects.

"We have to use this?" Shep said it would be easier for them to keep track of what was spent if they did that. "I can see that. However, this stuff that we're getting, do you think it would be cheaper to build a brand new building? I mean, this list has things on it like upgrading the bathrooms. Putting in new air conditioner units. I know for a fact that air units could run upwards of ten grand. Not that we could build for that much, but it would be costly."

"That's one of the things we're going to talk about. I've taken a look at the cost to build, as you suggest. However, the amount of red tape is a great deal to have to deal with. Even with Ricky helping me, he said it could take months to sometimes years to get approval for something like this. Then they could change their mind halfway through the project, and we're stuck." Rodney said he'd looked into things when he'd been told about the meeting today. "You finding out something that would help make this go easier is good with me."

"We build it on our own anyway. We can say that we're building it to use as a private school that we want to run for ourselves. Then once the building is finished, we can rent it out to the district, so they aren't responsible for the upkeep and maintenance of it. Also, we'd be able to upgrade when we want, as well as shut it down if it comes to that. I doubt we'll go that far, but it is something to think about." Heath said he liked Rodney's idea. "There's more, too, that Rebel and I were talking about. With the magic we both have, we can put things around the building inside and out that would make it safer for the kids. No one, not even the teachers, would have to be informed of it. But this magic we could put around it would simply be an added layer of protection for not just our children, but all of them."

"At what cost to you two? I mean, I don't have any kids right now, and I'm not in any kind of hurry to have them, but I also don't want the two of you hurt while keeping the kids that may or may not go there safe. What does it cost you in health?" Rebel told Heath it would only be something that they'd use when they were alerted to someone trying something. "So you'd have this like radar thing going on and would make it stronger when you felt a bad vibe. Or something like that."

"That's it exactly. No guns would be able to pass the front doors. Not even from the teachers. Also, there will be added protection on days like when pictures being taken. I know from being at the school on those days, it's a mad house. People coming and going. Rebel also suggested that we could do a tighter background check on anyone that enters the building. Not just the staff, but anyone." Heath was liking this more and more. "The cost of building the building would be better in the long run. However, having control of it and the things that would be going on with the building would keep us in the loop of knowing what is needed. We'd be able to have a firsthand look at all the upgrades when they're put in too."

"It's got my vote. I would like to suggest that we try to use as many local contractors as possible." Rodney told him he was looking into that as well. "Good. Then this list—should I try to find new things for the school or scrap it for something else?"

"We all have to agree on this. I don't want anyone thinking we have to do anything we're working on. If you don't want to be a part of the project or projects that we have going, that will be fine as well. Myself, I'm taking myself out of the police station project because I'm too close to the whole thing. If it were left up to me, I'd fire just about everyone on the force and start again. But that's just me." Heath asked Harris why that was. "I don't know, really. But if you were to take a look at the people working there, you'd see that most of them are older than I think is regulation for a force this size. Also, a great many of them are not just overweight, but they more than likely wouldn't be able to do their jobs if it became necessary. You might be saying we don't have to worry about that because we're a small town. But the moment we put in these improvements, we're going to have people wanting to come here simply because of the schools. It will become a problem then."

"I never thought of us growing and it causing trouble. I guess I just thought we'd be this quaint little town that we are forever." Rebel said there would be people coming to town for that reason too. They were a quiet town without much in the way of crime. "To be safer? Or to prove that we're not as safe as we had thought?"

"Both." That startled him. And while that was rolling around in his head, Rebel mentioned that there would be other beings coming as well. "They would know that Rodney and I are powerful. To kill us, which isn't possible, would be a big deal. Also, while I'm talking about immortality, we all have it. And with this magic, no one would be able to hurt one of the children, including the babies."

"I'm sorry, what?" Grandda looked around the room. "I thought we were all there anyway. That we'd not die for a long time. Are you saying it's changed in some way?"

"None of us will ever die. We can't be killed, and no one can harm us in any way. Nor can anyone, if they wanted to, remove our heads." Heath wanted to tell his grandda this was a good thing that Rebel was telling him, but she seemed to understand he was upset about this. When she sat next to him, taking his frail hand into hers, she spoke to only him. "Grandda, all you have to tell me is that you want to die, and I'll make it happen for you. I don't mean that I'll outright murder you, but I will be able to take the immortality from you whenever you wish. At any time you're ready. However, I'm hoping you wish to stay with us for a bit longer."

"I've been here a lot longer than I thought I would have been, honey. I do miss my wife and Jill Ann." She said she understood that. "I know you do. I surely do. Let me think on it a bit, and I'll talk to you some other time. All right?"

"Of course." Heath watched the two of them together. No one would ever think Grandda wasn't related to the women in this room by blood. They all looked a good bit like him, but it was the women that seemed to be as much a part of him as they were. Even with her red hair and dark eyes, Rebel looked like she could be his grandchild. "When more babies start coming along, I'm sure you'll be right there with them. Showing them the ropes like I'm sure you did for their fathers and uncles."

"I could get them in trouble when I wanted some fun. My wife would fuss at me, but I'd see her there taking a few pictures of them." He stood up and shook his head. "Dagnab it. I have some boxes of things I meant to bring up from the basement.

They're things your grannie made and put back for you all. There are some pretty little booties and baby things too. Not all of them blue. Like she knew there would be some little girls coming around. And I have a rocking chair for the lot of you too. I don't know how it was that we ended up with seven of them, but I got one for each of your homes. They got names with them too, so I'd make sure they went to the right person. And a handful of pictures of you being rocked in them by your momma, me, and your grandma. I wish I'd have remembered."

"We'll get them after this, Grandda. It'll be something I think all of us will want to talk to you about too." Grandda told him he'd enjoy that as well. "Did you make the chairs?"

"I didn't. I wanted to, but I was dealing with that stupid son of mine too much when you boys were little. But they're good ones. Chester Windchaser made them. I think he might still be around too. He is a wolf—one of the founding fathers, I think." Shep said he remembered them. They were very decorated with carvings. "That'll be them. I think for each of you, there was a different animal carved into them, with other hints of what you might grow into. Now that I think on it, Rodney, you have a stethoscope on yours."

Grandda told each of them what he thought was on their rocker. Heath had no doubt that Grandda knew exactly what was on them, and he'd bet he knew the date they'd been finished up too. Something that he'd learned about his grandfather in the last few months was that he was sharp as a tack and didn't suffer fools easily. Also, his job at the grocery store was getting him out more. Active. Heath loved the old man with all his heart and was hoping that any children he had would get to know him as well as he had.

Lunch was just grazing food, Shep called it. Heath had never had a lot of the things that were there, but he did enjoy trying them. His favorite so far was the little frittatas. He thought they were also delicious with the fresh guacamole. But there were other things he loved too. The pizza rolls were great. There were also tiny meatball subs and meat ones. As he was filling his plate up for the third time, he glanced up and saw that there was dessert as well.

Heath knew his brothers well enough to know they'd start on the desserts first if they were out there. Picking up an entire cherry pie, he asked Molly to please put it back for him to take home. She winked at him and told him she had six more in the freezer and that he was welcome to take two home with him for later. Happy that he'd seen the dessert tray, Heath filled his plate to overflowing.

"Who the hell are you eating for? Twins?" He laughed with Rodney. Then he told him about the desserts. "I saw them when I first got here. Molly already set me three of the carrot cakes aside. She's been baking all week, she told me."

"I love carrot cake." He said he did as well, and that was the reason he put it back. "You'll share, right? I mean, I'd gladly give you a cherry pie for one of your cakes."

The two of them were dealing about the cakes and pies when Grandda joined them. After telling him about the pies and cakes, Grandda went to the kitchen. He didn't know what he was up to, but he'd bet his last chicken wing that he was going to make out better than he and Rodney did together.

They were still standing around the food when Grandda came out of the kitchen. Christ, he nearly swallowed his entire handful of French fries when Grandda came out with a large platter of not just pieces of every pie that was going to be served, but cakes and a gallon of ice cream too. And he also knew that he'd not share. Grandda was the champion of pie eating — or whatever desserts were at the table. Kissing the man on the forehead, Heath told him how much he admired him. He also told him he hoped someday he had a kid that Grandda would take under his wing to show him how to con a collection of desserts from the cooks.

"It is an art form, I tell you." They were both laughing when he handed a slice of the pecan pie to Harris. Apparently, he'd share, but only with the women in the family. "You have me a couple of grandkids, Heath, and I'll make sure they know every trick I taught you when you were a little kid."

"Deal. I just have to find me a mate, that's all."

The rest of the meeting was gone over. The amount of money they were spending on a few of the projects scared him enough that he wanted to back off. He spoke to Harris about it.

"You don't have to worry about it, Heath. There is a great deal of money. And I'm good at investing as well. I want you all to know that even with all the projects we have going on and the ones that we're starting, it won't make a dent in what I've gotten. What *we've* gotten. Also, you'll each receive another credit card today that you're to use for something fun. I don't know the vampires that left it to me, but I'm sure they'd be thrilled to know we all enjoyed their savings very much." Heath asked her if she was going to do the same. "We are. We have, actually. Shep and I have ordered a motor home. One big enough that we can enjoy and have great vacations in. We've even gotten one big enough for our children that are coming, as well as Grandda, to come along with us. It'll be something we can do forever, I'm hoping."

He'd never been camping. Not even as a child. Of course, as his cat, he'd sleep out under the stars, but he didn't think that was the same thing. Thinking about how much he might enjoy taking a trip like that, Heath decided he'd do something like that as well. Maybe, he thought until he figured out if he would like it, he'd go small.

Nah, he thought. Go big or go home, his mom used to tell him. Smiling, thinking about what he might want to do with a camper, he decided that until his mate came, and even after, he was going to take his grandda with him on each and every trip. He surely did love that old man.

~*~

Shannon knew there was some sort of upset going on in the hospital, but she wasn't going to let it interfere with what she was doing there. Her momma was going to die. Every time she thought of that, her eyes would fill up, and she'd have to take long, deep breaths in and out until the hurt and pain of it moved to a place in her heart that she'd be able to let out later.

"What are you thinking about now?" Smiling at her momma, she told her she'd been thinking about the hospital. "Sure you were. And I'm a monkey's aunt. Honey, we all die. I just got myself an earlier ticket than most would have."

"Don't make light of this." She told her that if she didn't, she'd be a puddle of tears. "I know, but I don't want you to leave me. We had so many plans, you and I. I want those memories to have after you're gone."

"Let's change the subject. Why are you thinking about this place? It's been a nice hospital, don't you think? I mean, I've not had one lick of trouble here." She told her what she'd overheard in the cafeteria. "Oh. I'd not heard that. But then I don't have a lot of friends coming here to visit me and bring gossip to me. What have you heard?"

"That there was a shakeup with one of the nurses. I'm not sure what it was about, but I guess they lost about ten of them in one mass firing. Doctors too. Do you remember when we first came here that people told us about the Marshall family? I think they had something to do with it." Momma told her that the Marshall family was some sort of big deal. "Yes. I looked them up. They're filthy rich. I'm not sure what that means exactly, but that's what they've been called by a few of the nurses. Also, I guess there is some speculation that they're shifters. Cats."

"Filthy rich implies that a person's wealth is offensive. I have no idea why someone would take exception to someone being wealthy, but that's what it means. Thank goodness for crossword puzzles." Her momma did love to do puzzles. Of any kind. It was something she did even now, but it took her longer because she was so weak. "You're overthinking again."

"I know. It's just really painful to know you could have been doing puzzles at home. I feel like this trip out here might have made you worse." Momma told her what her opinion of the trip was. "I guess that is one way to look at it. At least we were at a place to take you when you got ill. It came over you so quickly."

"I know I've said this to you before, but it is what it is. I want you to realize something else, too. You're here with me, Shannon. You could have been off to college or some job. But we had planned to spend some good time together, and we are. I will remember this when I'm looking down on you

from Heaven, sweetie. You are my heart, my life."
Shannon didn't even bother trying to hide the tears
that fell this time. "If you continue to cry like that,
I'm going to be all wet too."

They were both crying when the nurse came
in to take her momma's blood pressure. When she
left, Momma closed her eyes and said she needed
a nap. Momma told her to go and get something
good to eat, and she'd be right there when she came
back. Shannon knew it wore her out quickly when
she tried to stay cheerful for her. Resolving to try
and be less teary, Shannon made her way to the
cafeteria to get herself something to eat.

Not that she had a lot of experience eating
in the hospital cafeteria, but she thought this one
was superior in what it served up. They not only
had a daily special that had been delicious every
time she'd gotten it, but there was a wide selection
of desserts too. Her favorite so far was the farmers
peanut butter pie. She didn't understand the title of
it, but it didn't deter her from having a piece daily
when she came in.

It was hard for her to realize she'd been here
only two weeks with her momma. It seemed a
lifetime ago when she'd had to pull off to the side of
the road when Momma started throwing up blood.

Not just a little either—a scary amount of it. The ambulance was there within minutes and rushed her momma away from her. Driving to the hospital the medics had given her directions to, her momma was already in surgery when she finally made it there.

After the doctor said the words terminal cancer, very little else got through to her mind. Her momma had it in her bloodstream, which meant it had spread all over her body. It had taken her momma two days to recover from the loss of blood and then a couple more days for her to be able to talk to her. They had both cried that entire first day. Then Momma had gotten over it and seemed to be all right with what her body was doing to her.

Sitting at the table by the window, Shannon watched a couple of black squirrels chase each other all around the open garden area. Someone had planted some beautiful flowers in the area, and they were happy enough to make her feel a little better by just seeing them. When a large tray was set on the other side of her, she looked at the elderly man who sat down with her.

"Howdy, Darlin. I saw you sitting here all by your lonesome and thought I'd keep you company. I like that pie myself. Don't rightly understand the farmer part of it—far as I know, farmers didn't eat peanut butter—but then I'll eat it no matter what it's called. My name is Sheppard, but everyone calls me Grandda. What's your name?" She told him. "Shannon is a pretty name. It is. Not as lovely as you are, but about there. You're here with your mom. I heard the nurses telling me what wonderful people the two of you are. I'm sorry about your mom, sweetie. I truly am."

"Thank you." She decided she would unload on this man. For whatever reason, when he sat down with her, she thought of him as someone she'd known forever. Friends were something she didn't have a great deal of, and he seemed to be one. "She's going to die. Cancer. When she got sick in my car, we were headed to Florida. To catch a cruise ship for three glorious weeks. Now I have to figure out a way for me to go on without her."

"You will. That's a given, honey. I lost two loves of my life. Thought for sure I'd not want to carry on either, but I got me some grandsons and their wives that sort of bullied me into getting on with life." He laughed. "Harris, my granddaughter-in-law, she's a bit on the blunt side. Told me she was going to bury me alive if I just kept sitting there. She was right. Mean, but right in me not living. Now I have me a bunch of great-grandbabies and more to come."

"It's just my momma and me. She had me when she was very young. Her parents kicked her out even though they knew she'd been raped." Looking at the squirrels again, she continued with her story. "I was born on her fourteenth birthday. In all that time, she's never once made me feel like I ruined her life. Or blamed me when her parents were willing to take her back if she were to get rid of me."

"Your mom, she sounds like a heck of a woman. Yessiree, a heck of a woman." Shannon told him she thought so as well. "My grandson and his wife, they're doctors. Rodney, he told me he hates telling people they got cancer. He told me they know it's going to take their loved ones from them. Even his wife, Rebel, she told me it's worse when it's a child that is sick with it. It's a terrible thing. I'm so sorry the two of you are going through this."

"I am as well." She realized she'd eaten everything on her plate and did feel a little better for it. "You're very good company, Sheppard. Thank you for listening to me whine. I do that. My momma told me that it's a fact of life that we all die, but that her ticket came up sooner than she'd like. But she's all right with it. I'm not, in case I was hiding it."

"You weren't. But you weren't whiney either. Sometimes you just need to get things off your chest, and I was here to help you along with that." She thanked him again. "No need for that. I'm glad I could be here for you. You were looking a little off your feed, and I decided to come to see if I could help you."

"You did. A great deal, as a matter of fact." The speaker buzzed, something she'd come to associate with an announcement. Waiting for the person to speak, she had a sudden feeling it had to do with her momma. "I have to go."

As she was racing toward the elevator, she heard the room number called with a code blue. Her heart felt heavy as she realized that not only was it her momma's room number, but a code blue could only mean one thing. Sheppard got on the elevator with her.

"I'm going with you. In the event you need me." Nodding, she was crying hard when the doors opened. Knowing she'd not be able to go into the room just yet, she stayed as close as they'd let her. "Darling, come over here. You're going to be in the way."

"She's dying, and she's all alone. I told her I'd be there, and I'm not. What am I to do, Sheppard?"

Sheppard did something for her that she would forever be grateful for. He took her hand into his and shoved his way into the room. The doctors were still working on her momma, but she took her hand into hers.

"I love you, Momma. If you're going to do this, it's okay with me. Just go on and be the best angel ever." The little blip on the machine over her head made a sudden loud noise. When the staff started to work on her again, she told them no. "She's ready. And I can't see her suffering anymore."

"Are you sure, honey?" She nodded at Sheppard when he spoke to her from behind. "Then they'll let her go in peace."

Sheppard spoke to the staff there, and they went out of the room one by one. The noise was cut off at one point, and she held tighter to her momma's hand. Talking to her, telling her what she'd had for lunch, was all she could think to say to her.

"I met the most incredible person while away. Mr. Sheppard. I don't know him very well, but he was there when I needed him to be. He also made it so I could be here with you now. I'm going to miss you so much, Momma." She cried harder then, not caring one bit if anyone was judging her. Looking around, the only other person in the room with her was Sheppard. "I don't know what I'm supposed to do now."

"You'll figure it out. And if you don't, I'll be right here for you." He smiled at her. "You go on now and have yourself a talk with your momma, Shannon. She can hear you. I just know it."

She did what he said, telling her about the things she was going to do the rest of the day. "I know we called that funeral home to have arrangements made, but I don't know if I have to call them or not." Sheppard told her the staff would take care of it by coming to get her. "Good. I showed you pictures of the pretty cemetery I found for you. I love the fact that it's so well taken care of. You'll be the envy of all the others with the pretty tree that shades your spot."

She spent another hour with her momma. The funeral director must have been friends with Sheppard because she heard him tell the older man that his family was good. When she was asked if she was ready, Shannon left the room and sat in the hall with Sheppard. Leaning on his shoulder, she cried again, wondering, as she had been lately, what she was going to do now that she was all alone.

"You must think I'm silly. I'm a grown woman, and I'm afraid like a little girl. But she's always been with me, and now I don't know what I'm supposed to do." He told her she'd get to living, just as he'd done. "You're right. Momma would be fussing at me if she were here now. She'd say, 'Shannon, get yourself up and going before I have to kick you around.' She never actually kicked me, but I understood that she would if I didn't. I'm going to miss her a great deal."

"Well, of course, you are. But here is what you and I are going to do. I've been talking to my family, and I'm to invite you to my grandson's home. We'll have a nice dinner, and you can bunk in my house. It's no trouble at all, so don't be thinking I'm going to let you out of it." Shannon didn't understand this connection she had with this man, but she trusted him. "Then sometime tomorrow, I'm betting you'll be able to go to Henderson's place and make them arrangements for your momma. You'll feel a good deal better by getting a good night's sleep and some homemade food in your belly."

"Why are you being so nice to me? You don't know me from anyone else." He said he understood her pain. "I guess you would. More than anyone around."

In the end, she went to the funeral home after they left the hospital. The man there, Mr. Henderson, told her that even though everything had been arranged and paid for, it would help him a great deal if she were to answer a couple of questions.

"She decided no service was to be held. Do you still want that for her?" She said she didn't know, and Sheppard told the man they'd be there for her. "Very good. Also, I have you on the list for the spot next to your mother, Shannon. As soon as I have any information on that, I'll give you a call. How long after the service are you leaving?"

"Right away. I need to get home and finish the things there that we left to make this trip." The thought of going back to their home was hard on her. "I don't have much to take care of there, but I'm thinking of coming back here. To be close to her. Is there anything around here that I could rent?"

"You let me have a look around."

She nodded and finished up making the rest of the arrangements. She'd not have to be back here until one tomorrow. Then the burial was right afterwards.

Since it was so late, Sheppard asked her for a ride home. Agreeing that she'd take him, she wondered what sort of home he lived in. If she didn't like it, she could always drive herself to a hotel. However, when she pulled up the driveway, the home in front of her looked like a luxurious five-star hotel. The house — no, mansion — was huge.

"You live here?" He told her with a laugh that his grandson did. "My goodness, Sheppard, this is a mansion. Do the others live like this?"

"Yes. They all have big houses. They need to get into gear and fill them up for me with babies, but I'm loving the ones I have now. Little Dru, you'll just love him to pieces." He got out of the car and was still talking as he went up to the front. "That there is my grandson, Rodney. That's his mate, Rebel. You'd not believe it, but she's—"

"You're Sheppard *Marshall*, aren't you?" He nodded at her and asked if that was a problem. "No. I mean, it's not a problem. But you're a very wealthy family. Like the richest in the entire world."

"That don't mean that we're any different than most people." Only the richest family in the world would think something like that. "You're going to come in, aren't you, child? I'd hate to have to send Rebel after you. She's a little bit of a mouthy thing, but I love her to pieces."

Shannon really didn't think she had a choice in the matter. When the couple came down the steps toward them, she thought she could make it to the car before they got to her. However, she didn't count on Sheppard taking her hand into his and dragging her toward them.

"I think there has been a little confusion." Rebel asked her what she thought was confusing. "I thought Sheppard here was going to let me bunk in his home, and it would be a normal home."

"You're going to find out, I think, that no one in this family is even remotely normal. Come on now, I have some tea for you or strong whiskey should you need that too. Later, the two of us will talk about what your future is and have a good time." She started to ask what her future had to do with anything, but she was in the most beautiful home she'd ever seen. "It is beautiful, isn't it? I love it here."

Shannon felt like the rabbit falling down the rabbit hole. As soon as she was able, she was going to smack herself in the head for being so trusting and then go back home. No one, not anyone she knew that had funds out the ass, was this nice— this generous. As soon as she could, Shannon kept telling herself, she was going to go to a hotel.

Chapter 7

Rodney was looking over the plans when Trenton joined him. The two of them had tried to get together twice now, and something had come up. He'd never realized how money could be so time consuming. Today he'd told his brother that he had to get the work started before fall and asked if he was able to meet him out there by the gazebo.

"I've been looking over paint colors. Not that I was going to have it painted any other color but white, but I'm telling you now, Rodney, there must be two thousand colors of white." They both laughed. "Not that many, but too many for me to just go in and pick a color. Because there are things like flat white, semi-gloss white, and so on. Christ, I just wanted to get a good color. Not have to be stressed out over it."

"I've been looking at the original plans for this place. Someone sometime in the past has enlarged it. The thing is only supposed to be ten feet wide. But it's about twenty now. Do you suppose that will matter to the women?" Counting off his steps, Trenton told him it was about twenty-five. "I can see that it would be wonderful to have it larger. Especially since Lach was talking about wedding pictures and such. But now that I see this, I'm thinking even that extra few feet might not fit the bill either."

"I was thinking the same thing. She wants benches up here too. As well as a band in the summer months. I can see it with ferns hanging from the loops here, but even that will take up more room than I think she's thinking she'll have." Trenton told him he'd contact her. "That way, she can make the decision as to how wide she wants it."

Rodney looked at the area they were allotted to work in. There used to be all kinds of pretty flowers around here—roses, if he didn't miss his bet. Now there was a great deal of trash lying around, as well as things on the floor of the gazebo that he didn't want to investigate too hard. As he was thinking of how it was going to look, he saw Grandda coming toward them.

"I saw the two of you making your way here. Whatcha doing out this late?" He told him they'd meant to get here earlier, but life got in the way. "I know that. I had me a hankering to go to get me a piece of pie today at the hospital cafeteria and met up with a little girl that lost her momma when we were talking. Poor thing. They were headed on a vacation, just the two of them. She's at your house now, Rodney."

"I met her. She's a very nice woman. A little overwhelmed, but very nice." Grandda said he'd be that way too. "I looked over her mom's notes, and she was very lucky to have been able to say goodbye to her family. She was riddled with cancer all over her body."

"Nasty stuff, that cancer." Rodney nodded and looked at his watch when Grandda told them he was going on back to the house. "I'll see you there for supper, won't I?"

"Yes. Trenton, do you—? Why are you shaking your head? I didn't even get the question out." Trenton said he was staying away from his house for a while yet. "Why? What have you done? Please don't tell me you pissed Rebel off. She could turn you into a sheep if you did. Remember that."

"Really?" Rodney shook his head while

laughing. "Smart ass. No, you have a single woman at your home, and I'm betting donuts to dollars she's going to be mine or Heath's mate. That's the way it's been working around here. I'm not ready. Not that I think it will matter when she does come along, but my home is not ready. More than half the rooms are empty now."

"So fill them up, you turd. That mate of yours won't care a fig if you're living on the street." Grandda pointed to him. "Your brother here, he's got himself a mate. I think he's enjoying that."

"I love her." Grandda told him he'd better or he'd kick his bottom. "I believe you would too. But having a mate is so much more than just being in love. It's a whole new world too. Friendship and love, I know now, go hand in hand."

"It sounds like it makes you sappy. No thanks. I'd rather wait until I'm Grandda's age before I think of looking for a mate. Someone to take care of me in my retirement age." Grandda slapped him on the arm before Rodney did. "Oh, that won't work either. We're never going to get old as dirt."

Rodney was still laughing at Trenton and Grandda as they made their way back to his house. True to his word, Trenton went home, but not before teasing Grandda about pretty women and pie. He wasn't quite sure why Grandda went to the hospital to get pie, but he'd been doing it for years now, and he wasn't going to get into a debate about there being a nice bakery not far from where they all lived.

"This little girl, she's thinking of moving back here when she settles up her mom's stuff. I don't know why, but I feel like she'd be better off staying with you and Rebel." Rodney said he was all right with that. Unless she wasn't. "I think she'll stick around. For a while, any who. But there is something about her that makes me want to take her under my wing and help her out."

"Are you thinking she is one of the other two's mates? Rebel thinks the same thing. Or she knows. It's hard to tell with her sometimes. She told me she can see a bit into the future, but not much more than that. I can't, which I think I'm grateful for."

"Yeah, I thinking knowing too much would be hard to take." They were at the house then, and Grandda asked him if he'd sit a spell with him. Sitting in the rockers, they sat there in silence for several minutes until Grandda started talking. "I miss your mom. Everyday. I have a hole in my heart, too, from when your grannie passed on. I've been thinking about this living forever thing, and I want you to tell me truthfully if you were me, nearly ninety years old, would you want this thing?"

"Can I ask you a couple of questions first?" Grandda nodded at him. "All right. What does your age have to do with you being around forever? You're not sick. You're clear-minded, a great deal more than men half your age are. You don't seem to have any kind of soreness that keeps you from walking every day. Hanging out with the Forster kids when they're playing street hockey."

"That's a good question, and you're right. I'm fit as a fiddle. I do play around with them kids on account'a their daddy being out of the picture. They talk to me—trust me, they told me. So that's a plus. But as for my age? I don't know what that has to do with me being around either. What's your next question?" Rodney told him. "You see, that's all I can think about. Seeing my grandbabies being born. Growing up and becoming something. Seeing you boys coming to your own too. That's a good one. I talk to your mom and grannie when I get out there. They understand, I think, that I'm building up stuff to tell them. I know it seems silly, me taking pictures and showing them to the headstones there."

"Grandda, I think it's wonderful that you share them with Mom and Grannie. I believe that they see them. Being around Lach and the others, I believe a great many things I didn't before." Grandda said that was right. "I love so many things about having you here. I love too that you come and stay with each of us for a while. Hang out with our mates. They love you as much, if not more, than we do. And I know that Bella's dad is only thriving because you go there and talk to him."

"He's a good man. But he won't be hanging around me too much longer. The dementia, it's taking its toll on him. I see it more and more of late." Rodney knew that as well. Bella and his brother were looking for a place for him to live that was safer for him. "The other day when he got out of the house was the breaking point for Bella. He'd broken his hand and some fingers trying to knock out a window in a car he thought was his. She cried for nearly an hour after he was found because she'd not been able to keep him safe. I told her it wasn't her fault, but there was no helping her. That's when they decided to find him a safe home to live in."

"She asked me for some places I would send him to. I don't know what she'll do when he's out of the house. And I know that Dru will miss him. Even as young as he is, he lights up when he sees you and Fletcher coming to him." Grandda said he loved that little man. "It shows too. Rebel and I are waiting to get some of this magic that we have under control before we bring a baby into the mixture. It's scary enough having this much power. The probability of having a child as strong as we are is huge. I want to know what I'm doing before I have to try and figure out what an infant might be able to do."

"Are you two going to sit out here all evening, or do you think you could come in and join us for dinner?" Rodney kissed Rebel when she scolded them. "Grandda, you're a bad influence on Rodney. The trouble the two of you get into is growing daily. Did you get the things worked out with the gazebo?"

"Grandda said we should go with not just white, but a couple of other colors too. Like a tan and a nice shade of cream. That'll be nice colors for whoever wants to use it." Rodney followed Rebel and Grandda into the house as he continued. "Trenton thinks that since we have the original plans, we should use them, then make an extension off the back of it that's much larger. Wider and taller, I was thinking. He seems to think that with the idea of using it as a backdrop for photos, they'll need the extra room there."

"I love that idea." After they were all seated

at the table, he noticed that Shannon wasn't joining them. "She's sleeping. With my help. I don't think she's slept all that much since they arrived here two weeks ago. A good night's sleep will make her feel better about everything. At least I believe it will."

"That's a good thing you did for her, Rebel. I thought she was looking a little peaked too." Grandda poured himself some tea as he told them about his plans for the money he'd been given. "I think I'd like to see a bit of the world. I've not been anywhere special in a long time. I don't know if I'd want to camp it a little or not, but it's an option. Also, as a senior, I get a good discount on air travel, as well as ships, should I want to go that way."

"I love that idea." So did Rodney, and he told him that as well. "You'll need to have a good camera to take lots of pictures you can send to us all — also, a passport. I'll see how to go about that. Unless you already know."

"Nope. I've never had the occasion to need one, so I've not the foggiest on how to make that work. Thank you, Rebel. That'd be really helpful. I was going to see if Rodney here could help me pick out some luggage. The stuff I have is older than any of you people." Rodney told him he'd love to help out. "I knew you would. Well, let's eat this here fine meal. I got some figures to work on with my paying job money."

Rodney knew he'd hired five men to help with the grocery part of his business. They would go shopping for someone and then take it to them. They were also, from what he'd heard, making good tips, something no one had thought of. Also, Grandda had set up a few men, younger than the others, to shovel snow from driveways and walkways. Grandda was having people clamoring to work with him. And twice that many people asking for their help. Yet another reason to feel proud of his grandda.

When dinner was over, they settled in the living room. It wasn't yet chilly enough to have a fire, but he could tell that Rebel wanted one. The house had free gas to it, so burning the fireplace didn't cost anything. It just created a little too much heat. As soon as he had it on and was seated again, Rodney looked over at his grandda. The man was sound asleep.

"He ordered the roses to be put in next year. They were your mom's favorite, he told me. There is also wisteria that will be planted that will be in full bloom in a few years. Less if I were to help it along." They both watched Grandda snore softly. "I've been looking around town, and I think there are a lot of improvements that can be made that won't cost the bank. I know there is supposedly a lot of money, but we don't need to replace everything when the older stuff is still good enough. Not good enough, I guess, but it's weathered this town this long, so I'm sure that it'll last for a good long time."

"That's what we were talking about at the gazebo. Grandda suggested that we use the wood we're going to have to take down for some park signs. You know, keep out of the flowers and such. He also suggested we could put the names on them for the people that donated over a hundred dollars. He said more people would help out if they could see their names in print." Rebel laid her head on his shoulder. "How is Shannon doing? I mean, she was pretty upset when I saw her today."

"She's doing well. I had her talking about her mom before she went up to rest. They were incredibly close, the two of them." Rodney said that was what Grandda had told him. "I think that once she rests, she'll be able to handle just about anything thrown at her. I offered for one of us to go with her when she has to sort through her mom's things. I would think it would be difficult for her."

At some point, they both must have dozed

off because when their phones rang, they were both startled awake, and he was tossed off the couch. Answering his phone, when Rebel walked out of the room with hers plastered to her ear, he heard yelling and cursing right off.

"Doctor Marshall, I would like for you to come to a house for a woman that has been beaten nearly to death." The officer at the other end gave him the address even as Rodney was pulling on his shoes. He asked if he was all right, as his voice was strained and full of anger. "No. No, I'm not. We're waiting on you so that we can make the charges go either way for Mr. Todd. Murder or attempted murder. There is also an unborn child."

"I'm on my way. There are children in the house, I'm assuming that's why you've called my wife too?" He said it was, and they were beaten up pretty badly as well. "I'm on my way."

Just as Rebel came into the room, he started for his bag when she handed it to him. Telling him that she was taking them there, he closed his eyes and held onto her. They were standing right outside the house when he opened his eyes. Kissing her on the mouth, quickly, they headed to the front door opening and then into what he thought was the kitchen area.

There were broken pieces of furniture all over the room. Plates and glasses were broken and lying in a dangerous way on the broken furniture and other items there. Blood was mingled in with all the mess and made the room look like it was a strange and macabre art attempt. There, lying in the middle of all of it, was a woman so badly beaten she didn't look human at all.

"He beat her." Mr. Todd started laughing, lunging at Rodney and telling him not to touch his woman until he was finished with her. "The neighbors called it in. When we arrived, he was ready to take an axe to her head."

"Telling me that she's not going to birth me a son. I done got me two fucking girls that she won't let me sell off. Fucking cunt should just die." No one said a word as Rodney, ignoring the man, felt for the pulse of the woman. "I hope to fuck she's alive. I want to have another go at her. She's a lying fucking bitch, and she'll learn that I mean business."

"I'm reasonably sure she understood that." He looked at the officer. "I'm sorry, she's passed on. I'm going to work on saving her child. I can hear the heartbeat, and it's going to be next if I can't save it."

"Please save one of them." Nodding, he pulled out the tools of his trade and did something he always did in his practice—he told the patient what he was doing. Rebel joined him in the room, and Officer Layman asked about the children. "When we arrived here, they were huddled in the corner over there. Bleeding and in obvious pain. Never said a word to anyone as we separated them from the mess in here."

"They're going to the hospital now. I let them out through the bedroom window so they'd not see what is going on in here." Rebel looked at him. "You can do this, Rodney. I'll assist you in any way I can."

Nodding, Rodney set to work to deliver the child by C-section. Pulling the little girl free of her mother, Rodney handed her off to Rebel. She was tiny, much smaller than he thought she should be for a newborn. He wasn't sure how far along Mrs. Todd had been, but the baby looked to be fully developed. When Rebel told him to get the other child, he was dumbstruck for a few seconds.

There're twins there, Rodney. Take the other child before he dies. There is a good chance we can save them both if you hurry. He did so. Freeing the second child, he could see that he was slightly heavier than his sister. But the newborn wasn't responding to any of the stimuli to get him to breathe. *Give him a little of yourself. I cannot stand the fact that in addition to losing their mother, those little girls are going to lose a sibling as well.*

Rodney wasn't entirely sure how to do it, but he just did what came naturally to him. He told the little boy to live. Almost as soon as the word and the magic left his body, the child screamed out his first breath of air, like he'd only been waiting on someone to tell him to.

"That's my son." Rodney was cleaning up the little boy while his sister was having the same done by Rebel. Ignoring Todd was the best thing he could think of doing since he was bragging that he was going to raise himself a boy finally. Rodney noticed that the baby boy and girl were both bruised. The boy also had a wound on his left thigh that looked like a gunshot wound. "He's going to be just like me."

"Christ, I hope not. Having just one of you around is bad enough." Rebel looked at him. *Tell Layman what you suspect happened to the baby. It will lengthen that monster's stay in jail. I've already told him that I believe the beating of the mother has hurt the little girl.*

"This is what I think is a gunshot wound here on his leg. I'll have to stitch it up and hope the bruising doesn't cause him any long-term trouble." Layman had one of the other officers take pictures. Not just of the wound, but both children as they were laid on their mother's body. "If you don't need anything else with us, I'd very much like to get these two to the hospital and have them checked out. Also, you'll need to call the coroner. He'll need to get her to the hospital as well."

As they were leaving with the second ambulance, he and Rebel worked with the babies, taking their temps and weighing them, even going as far as to measure them for their length. Both were doing much better now, but he was worried that once they were a few hours older, the bruising on the little girl's head might cause her some issues. But they'd have to wait to get some X-rays before he would know anything.

"They wanted me to tell you that Todd is in jail." The driver of the ambulance, he couldn't remember his name right now, told them both. He told him he was sorry and asked after it. "Basil Basken. My mom thought that having an herb name would ward off the devil. I didn't have any tempting very much, so I'm thinking she did right. I asked Layman about the gunshot wound he had in his shoulder, and they said he could suffer until tomorrow. That the two of you had your hands full with the children. One of his men shot Todd so he'd not use the axe on the missus."

"Have you been called to that home often?" Rodney looked at Rebel when she asked. It was something he never did when on a call, asking for personal information that didn't pertain to his job. Basil told her it was at least twice a week and also to the school when the children showed up beaten. "Someone should show him how it feels to be beaten like he did those little girls."

Rodney hadn't seen the children. Rebel had not just sent them ahead to the hospital but had also ordered a lot of tests to be done, as well as putting them in the same room. Having them stay overnight was the best way to calm them. Rodney wondered what was going to happen to the babies when there was no one to take them.

I've got some information on the family if you'd like to have it. Rodney asked Harris if it was bad news. He couldn't take anymore tonight. *I don't blame you. I'm so sorry that you lost her. She was, according to those that knew her, a very nice woman that had it bad with her husband. Or who they thought was her husband. He wasn't, just so you know. Not legally anyway. Also, just a heads up, the other two do not have Todd's name on their birth certificate. I'm looking into how that happened, but until I do, their last name is the same as their mother's was. Avery.*

> Tell me what you know. But kindly tell me the bad shit with a few good things sprinkled into it. I'm telling you now, I don't think my heart could take much more. The little boy I'm holding right now not only lost his mom, but the man who killed her was his father. He's been shot and beaten up, and he's not even an hour old.

She told him again how sorry she was. *I am as well. These little ones are going into the system, aren't they?*

I don't know how to answer that. There is a great aunt that might take them, but I'm doubting the courts will allow her to. She's in her late sixties. Also, Belinda, the mother, has a sister and a brother that I know of. The brother is in the service, married with four kids of his own. The sister is off the grid. I'm not sure where she is, but I'll find her.

He asked her what off the grid meant. *She's a ghost. No working social security number, no address. No job that I can find. She doesn't have any credit cards, no utilities. There is a post office box number for her in this town that I've found, but according to the people there, Belinda is the one that gets the mail out of it and goes through it. Then I guess she sends it to another P.O. box in another state. So far, I've found nine more of those that someone sends off to another address. Could be she's in the service as well and being moved a great deal, or she's hiding from someone.*

But you don't think that's the case, do you? Either of those ideas? Harris told Rebel that for some reason, it didn't feel right. *I remember my mom telling us if it doesn't feel right, then it's not. With you, that would go double. What is it you think she does?*

What I was doing.

Well, there was a lot to be said about that, but they were pulling into the hospital now, and he no longer had the time to speak to her. After telling her what he was doing, Harris told him she'd get back with him.

Sheila met them at the nursery department. She was going to assist Rebel in whatever she needed to do with the little girl. Adaline had shown up too, but she was working in the overcrowded emergency room, and he told her that if she didn't mind, it would be good for her to help out. There had been a wreck on the highway just out of town, and they weren't sure what to expect yet.

The little boy had been quiet since he'd given out his first lusty cry. After getting him cleaned up better, then diapered, he looked to be doing well. The five stitches in his thigh were photographed, then sent to the police, along with his paperwork as to what had happened to him. By the time he was finished up, Rebel came to see him.

"She's doing fine now that she's had a bottle. Belinda's doctor has been notified, and he told me what the plans had been for the children when they were born. It was just a staff employee, he told me. Belinda didn't have a preference, he told me, other than someone who would be kind to the babies." He asked her if she thought Belinda knew she was having twins. "She did. And she purposely kept that part out of her conversations with Todd. Also, she was running when she went into labor. The other two were going to be staying at a neighbor's home until she could come back for them. That was the reason Todd's name was never put on the certificates. So he couldn't claim them in the event she was able to get away. I have an idea what I want to do with some of the money Harris is going to give us for projects. I want to purchase the old high school and turn it into some sort of home for pregnant women. There won't be a mention of how we'll help them get out of a bad relationship or help them get away. It would just be a clinic of sorts to help mothers have a safe delivery and leave the place when they are able. There will be daycare as well for other children, so they can run as well."

"I'm sure it's not as simple as that, but I think that's an excellent idea — especially the daycare part for the other children. I've run into trouble with that a couple of times when the mother couldn't find a sitter for them, and they had to sit in the waiting room alone. Mostly because the father couldn't be trusted to take care of them. Terrible situation to get into if you ask me." She smiled at him. "Once word gets out that we've assisted in only one of the women and her children getting away, no one will allow their pregnant women to go there."

"I've thought of that too. I'm working on that as we speak. The police could help us, and I know Harris would as well if we ask. I want this to work." He said he did as well. "Good. That'll be all we need. Cooperation."

As he set up the care for the twins, he thought of very little else but the woman dying like she had. To be carrying a man's child and him thinking she had any say at all over whether it was a girl or boy. Men needed to have a lesson in how that worked. Telling them that the male was the parent that contributed the chromosome that decided that part would perhaps save a lot of fights between a man and a woman. Then he thought that no one would believe him, especially not the type of person that would believe that the woman had the determining gene.

Heading down to the pediatrics floor, he picked up the file on the girls. They were both hurting, he'd been told, and had needed stitches, but they were in generally good health. After getting a good meal into their bellies, the nurses on duty said that they'd gone to sleep on their own. He was glad. Rodney wanted to be able to save everyone he worked on. It had taken him a very long time to get it in his head that there wasn't any way to save them all. It didn't mean that he didn't try, but it was an impossibility that he wished was different.

Chapter 8

James watched his target as they moved all around the restaurant. He wasn't there to end her life, such as it was, but to get her to a safe house, then go to his own home. There were all sorts of things she was going to be charged with, one of them treason to her own country. When someone sat across from him, he nearly snarled at his sister. Instead, afraid of her, he just ate his soup like he'd been expecting her all along.

I'm here to take over. He didn't bother looking up at her. The link they shared had it so that they'd have to never speak out loud if they didn't want to. *Someone has called your boss and said something has happened at your house, and you need to be transported home. Billy broke his leg in a fall from the bleachers at the football field at home.*

By the way she worded it, he knew that not only was there nothing wrong with his son but that she'd already checked it out. When a bowl of the same soup he was sipping was set in front of her, she did what he'd done when he'd gotten his. Paige not only checked it for poisons but also smelled it to find out as well. When she pushed it away, he did as well, and unlocked the clip on his gun and put his hand on it at the ready.

Why were you called, do you know? She shrugged. Something she knew he hated, and she did anyway. *What's going down here? Anything I've done, or you?*

Both of us, as a matter of fact. She was eyeing the room, and he didn't bother looking too. Something he'd learned a very long time ago about his little sister, she was fucking good at her job. So was he, but he was too cautious, as he'd been told by her several times a day. *There are two geeks over by the door. They're trying their best to blend in, but they're not fooling anyone. Their language is too perfect, and they're dressed like peasants. Peasants can't afford bottled beer or the food they're eating. Not at the same time, anyway.*

Glancing in that direction, he took in as much as he could in the way of information. She was right, as usual—they were trying hard to blend. Also, he noticed that four other men were watching them and making no bones about how they didn't like them being there. He thought they were KGB but doubted he was right on that. The Soviet Union had nothing to do with this area, and the *Komitet Gosudarstvennoy Bezopasnosti* weren't the type to carry knives when guns were going to be needed.

"I think they're Feds. It would be just like them to come in and fuck up my day when I had such plans for the evening. Getting laid is far more fun without having someone firing over your head in a sleazy hotel room. Don't you think?" He just grunted at her. When she smiled, he wanted to laugh with her, but one of the Feds moved. "They're just going to walk right up to us and give all our hard work a day off too. Mother fuckers. Why is it that one hand, them, never knows what the other hand, us, is doing? Oh well. I'm going to bounce before they get here."

Sure enough, the man came and sat down in the chair his sister had only just vacated. Not removing his hand from the gun he had in his hand now, James looked around the room and then into the eyes of the man he was going to have to kill if he had fucked this up for him. Asking him in Russian what he wanted, the man didn't even know the local language.

"I asked you what the fuck you're wanting by coming in here. You should be sitting behind a desk and pushing shit around that you think you might be doing correctly. What do you want?"

"I have a message from my boss that I'm to tell you." He didn't bother with asking the man who his boss was or even what the message might have been about. Wanting him gone, he looked slightly over the man's shoulder and into the eyes of his sister. The gun she put in the back of the Fed's head looked like she was trying her best to make it stay there forever.

"You're in my seat, moron." She spoke French to him. Even he could see he didn't have a clue on how to answer her. Then she tried any number of other languages she knew, which in his estimation was about all of them. "Who the fuck would send you into a war zone without you knowing a single language other than English? I am taking a fucking big chance here in thinking you might well know that one, but who the hell knows? What is it you want, jerk off? You have less than five minutes to tell me."

He didn't even get that long. Someone darkened the door to the shabby little shithole they were in and tried to kill everyone in there. James grabbed the woman he'd been there for when she'd been shot and let his sister fend for herself. He knew as well as Paige did that she had a better chance of getting out alive than anyone else. James was running down the row of houses behind the restaurant when he heard from her next.

"Is she dead? Should be, I'm thinking, for all the shit she's caused here." He leaned against the tree with the girl still on his shoulder and laid her on the ground. Checking her pulse, he told Paige she was alive. "Good. The Feds are all dead. Not only dead, but they were stupid enough to have worn their badges around their necks so anyone could see what a prize they got by killing them. I'm going to call their CO. Their commanding officer, or whoever the fuck is their boss, should have known better than to send idiots like this here. What did he want?"

"Don't know. Don't care. Where are you?" She told him. "How the fuck did you get up there? I'm assuming you know people that know people."

He laughed when she did, but he knew that to be true. Had it not been for Paige, he would have died a long time ago. As it was now, even getting injured was only a quick shift away from not being an issue again.

Paige had joined the service two weeks before he had. They had both gone through boot camp at the same time, but he hadn't seen her after the first couple of months there. James had thought she'd flunked out. But it had been her excelling in so much of the shit they had been teaching them that had gotten her looked at for more serious work than just a man with a gun.

I need for you to do something for me. He told her anything. *You still have a couple of contacts back home? I mean, someone you can trust more than you do me?*

I don't trust you at all, so that'll be easy. When she didn't laugh, he asked her what was going on. *I read the Fed's mind. You check in with your contact and let me know what they tell you.*

Should I be worried? She told him she was calling the CO of the other men. Not at all answering his question. *Really? Is that necessary, you think?*

I do. I'm hoping the Fed was wrong, and this was just another attempt to get you alone. He was beginning to worry now. When Paige told him to get back to her, he did something he'd never done in all his life—reached out for another person other than his sister.

Mr. Marshall? My name is James Avery. Can you give me some answers about what is going on there?

The man broke down. James, unsure of what was going on, knew it had to do with his other sister and her little family, and he sat down. The car that was going to meet him here pulled up and took the woman away. *What's happened? Tell me, please?*

Your sister, Belinda Avery, she passed on a few days ago. James didn't know what to say but did ask if it had been Todd. *Yes. She was carrying his children when he beat her and those little girls of hers. My grandson — you might remember, he's a doctor — did all he could to save them babies. She had herself a little girl and a boy. Todd, he's in jail for attempted murder and murder. More to that, but I'm not privy to it right now.*

She's really dead? Mr. Marshall said he was powerful sorry about it but that she was gone. Had been buried just today. *I can't come home right now. I will, but I'm out of the country. I'll send my wife and family there to get things taken care of while I'm working on coming home. Thank you for getting her buried. Who's caring for the children?*

My family is right now. We didn't want them to be put in the system. Not that they might not end up there anyway, but for now, they're safe as hens' eggs in a nest. He loved the way Mr. Marshall had spoken. *You get yourself home here, and we'll hold off as much as we can. The house and its contents are being locked up. The murder, it happened at the house, you see. The little ones, the other two girls, they've been knocked around too, but they're going to be all right. I don't suppose you know where your sister is, do you?*

I'll find her. Mr. Marshall told him that would be good. *I'll be home in a week or less if I can get enough strings pulled. I haven't any idea if my sister will or not. She travels to a beat of her own drums.*

Yes, while I don't remember her much, I know all about someone doing their own thing. You let me know if I can help you with those there strings, James, and I'll see how hard they need to be pulled. All right? He told him he'd be fine. *You will be. I know it. I'll see you when you arrive. And let me know when you figure out your wife and family. We'll be putting them up, too, so you don't have to worry about that.*

After closing the connection, he sat there for a little while longer. Belinda was dead. Murdered by a man that all of them had hated. Now she had four children too, ones he'd never met in the first place. Looking up when a shadow fell over him, he saw Paige. Putting out her hand, he let her help him up from the ground. James started to tell her what he'd found out.

"Not here." Nodding, he followed her

through the town for what seemed like miles. When they happened upon a house just outside the city limits, the two of them went in, and he was startled at not only how lovely the little home was but that it was air-conditioned. Looking at Paige, he asked her what was going on. "This is one of my hidey holes. Might as well be comfy when the bad guys are after your ass. Don't you think?"

"She's gone." When she nodded, he wondered who she had spoken to but didn't ask. Paige, like him, had contacts all over the world. Knowing about a sister in bumfuck Ohio, would be an easy thing to check out. "I'm going home. After I speak to Sara, I'm going to follow her there to find out what happened. Butch Todd killed her."

"He won't be anything anyone has to worry about soon enough." James didn't bother asking her. It would do him no good and only serve to piss her off. "I can't leave yet. I have two things going at once here, and I have to see them through. I don't know what I'd do there anyway but to kill Butch. He's going to die anyway, but that's all I can offer you at the moment."

"I understand." He did understand, better than most did, about his sister. "I was going to call Sara. Perhaps she can get us there and back without any issues."

When Paige left him standing there, he looked around the room. This was a room for a woman who didn't kill for a living. It was soft — the earth tones of the room suited his sister well. When she returned with a handful of money, he asked her where she'd gotten it.

"My stash. I don't get paid by check, as you know. I don't have a bank account other than the one that is in town for Belinda to use when she needed it. So I just stash it here. Other places too, but it's here when I need it." He looked at the stack. There were ten bundles of one hundred dollar bills. "It's a hundred grand. Just use it instead of your credit card. That way, no one will know where you've gone when you leave here."

"I could buy my own plane if this is all real." She didn't take the bait, nor did she give him any shit when he asked her how he was supposed to get around with this much cash. "What is it, Paige? I've given you ample lead way into busting my chops, but you've not bitten."

"The men that were sent to find you. They were sent by Harrison Parker." James sat down hard but didn't say anything. "She's in the FBI now. I called to speak to someone in charge of the two idiots that were here, and they told me that would be Agent Marshall. It didn't take me long to find out who she was."

"Marshall? You mean she's connected with the Marshall family of jags?" She only had to nod, and he felt blindsided once again. "How the hell did she get that gig? For that matter, how did we not know about this before? I thought we had enough tags on her to keep her in our sights forever?"

"I don't know, to be honest. I didn't talk to her, but I could have. I should have, actually." She looked at the doorway into a part of the house he couldn't see into. "I will, as a matter of fact. But here. Where I know she can't find me."

He didn't have to ask her what she meant. James knew Paige well enough to know that if she told you no one would find her, no one would. Ever. He knew too that even if a person were walking right over her, they'd never know she was right there beside them until it was too late. Looking at the money again, he wondered what was going to happen next. Because something was always about to go down while they were dealing with bad situations in their line of work.

By the time he was ready to go back onto the streets, he not only had a way back to the States, but he had two months off with pay. Whoever his sister had contacted on his behalf, they had fallen all over themselves getting him home. James asked her if she was going to be all right.

"I could have killed him six months ago. He was right there in my sights, and I could have blown his fucking head off, and no one would have been happier about it than me." He asked her what had happened. "Belinda. She asked me not to do it. Said that it would haunt her if I did. I told her he was going to kill her someday, and she told me that it was her lot in life. But that if he would die now, by the gunshot to the head, she'd lose her babies because no one would ever believe she'd not killed him."

That was true. Belinda had been trying her best to leave Butch for years. The man would drag her back every time, hurting her and the girls more each time. When Paige told him to go, to be careful, he knew she'd have to deal with this on her own. Paige would carry the guilt to her grave if she really thought it had been her fault their sister was dead because of something she'd not done when she could have.

~*~

Harris was looking over contracts she should

have done days ago to purchase the land they were going to build on. Also, they were going to purchase the surrounding acreage. That way, if necessary, they could expand as much as they wanted. She had a feeling they'd have a mob on their hands once word got out what they were doing. When her phone rang next to her, she picked it up without looking at who it might be. "Hello, Harrison Parker. But I guess you go by Agent Harrison Parker Marshall now, don't you?" The voice. Because she did know it and not the person on the other end of the call, it terrified her in ways she could not deal with right now. "If they put you in charge of sending your men to other countries, I might just have to tender my resignation as an American citizen. Christ, they were all killed, as well as about half a dozen civilians. Stupid rookie mistake, Harrison. Even for you."

"I didn't send anyone out of the country." The laughter was like nails going down a chalkboard, devoid of humor and full of spiteful hatred. "What happened? Perhaps then I can send someone to you, and you can train them on—"

"They couldn't even speak the language. Who does that? You apparently. Stupid woman. Some of the people in that place were parents with children and had someone to go home to nightly." She asked again what she was talking about. "They spoke of finding a man by the name of Avery. That was just before they were blasted away by some men who don't take kindly to American service men being so close to their families. Last or first name? I haven't any clue. But killed they were because no one taught them any kind of rules of engagement when taking down a person."

"I didn't send anyone there." She pulled up her satellite computer and looked to see if she could capture a location on the caller. "Why don't you give me your name, and we'll have a nice lunch at my expense."

"No. Why do you think I'm going to go anywhere that you are? I'm not. So leave it alone."

Harris moved around to the last location she had, and then the computer bounced her to a different country, as well as five or six places in that region. "You're bouncing. I guess I would be better off just giving up on trying to find you."

"You say that, but I know for a fact that you're not stopping. You're too pig-headed and stupid to think anyone is smarter than you." Harris watched the IP address jump all over the world. It even repeated the same place several times before the few seconds it would take her to make the identification a hit. "I have their wallets. That would cause a great deal of trouble for you should they have been found with their badges on. Also, you might want to remember this for the next time you send out bunnies, that—"

"Bunnies?" She told her what she meant by that. "All right. I guess that's as good a description as I've heard. Soft and cuddly, but worthless when it came to having any idea how to get away. But I swear to you, I did not send anyone to wherever happened."

The voice gave her the location using longitude and latitude. Since Harris had access to the satellite in the sky, she put in the numbers, and the camera zeroed right in on the restaurant. She was still looking it over when the voice spoke again.

"Fifteen people died there. A loss of income for an entire family. The people working there, they were helping a family of eight when you blasted their place." Once again, she told her she'd not done it. "Then who?"

"I'm looking now. I swear to you on the life of my unborn child that I had nothing to do with this. Nothing. I'm seeing who did it right now. I am looking for a man by the name of Avery. His sister has been murdered, and I need for him to come home." Harris didn't wait for the voice to speak again when she spoke to her about the murder. "The children are as safe as we can make them. The newborns are coming along nicely for being born three weeks earlier than they were due. But— Jesus H. Christ, the place is gone."

"Someone came in the middle of the night and made sure no one was able to get anything from clues that might have been left behind. Standard protocol here. Bodies were still in there when the place was demoed. You might well want to remember that if what you say is true and someone sends in troops that aren't ready for their work."

Harris knew in some countries, they did make sure there wasn't evidence when Americans were killed. But this wasn't one of those places. And the bodies would have been burnt beyond any reasonable recognition, not to mention so hot there would be nothing left to ID them with.

"I need your help with this. First of all, I'd like to get the IDs of the victims that were there from my end. After that, I'm thinking I can narrow it down to see where I have to look next." Voice told her it wouldn't work. The men, five of them, didn't have any idea of what happened other than it was her that sent them. "You can read minds. You're a shifter, then. Are you being safe?"

"Not that it matters a hill of beans to you, but I'm nearly never safe." Harris couldn't help it, she burst out in laughter. She felt the touch of someone in her mind. Harris could have blocked the person, but she thought that Voice would trust her more if she were to let her find what she wanted. "What do you know of a man by the name of Lakeside? He's a colonel. I don't know what branch, but he's been mentioned a few times around the place that was taken."

"The only Lakeside I know is Patty. I don't think I ever heard that he was in the service or not. Why are you asking?" No answer, but she did give her a social security number. "Hang on, I'm pulling it up now."

Harris closed out the program for trying to find Voice. Putting in the social, she got seven hits on it right away. With four of them, there were even pictures to go with the numbers. Looking at them side by side, she could tell it was the same man, but he was changing his hair color just enough where he might have been mistaken for Lakeside.

"The same person has been using the number since numbers were given out. The first time he got it, he said he was nearing sixty." She told Voice she could see that. "Also, if you'll notice, he's aging himself. Or he looks really good for being nearly one hundred and fifty years old. There are only a few shifters that can do that with any amount of success."

"Vampires and witches." She thought about telling her she knew a witch but decided she more than likely knew that. Voice seemed to be one step ahead of her on a great many things. "This person, Avery, do you know him?"

"Would you believe me either way?" She told her she would. Definitely. "Maybe. I don't trust you any more than I can toss you. And I'm pretty good at tossing shit out when I've no use for it. Just like you were before getting fat with a kid."

There wasn't anything in her voice that told her shit. No accent that she could determine. There were no words she used that Harris could pick out that were hers alone. No hint as to where she might be at any given second. Pulling up the search for the IP address that she was calling from had hit seven thousand places so far and was still chasing her. Fuck. Harris hated the unknown.

"I tell you what, Agent Harrison. You find out what is going on with the restaurant, and I'll do something nice for you." Harris asked her how nice. Would she give her a name to work with? "Never. Unless I need something major from you. Which I'm thinking will never happen between the two of us."

"You don't know that. We could be besties." The laughter again, devoid of anything other than just the sound of it. "I'll do you a solid, Voice. You need me for anything, and I'll move heaven and earth to get whatever it is. Even if it's coming to pick you up because your ass is blown to shit."

"Yeah? Even though you don't trust me?" She told her once again that she did, for some reason she didn't have an answer for. "I might take you up on that, Agent. I might just. I have a couple of major jobs coming up, and I'm hoping that I get my ass blown to shit anyway. But if I change my mind, you'll be the first that I call."

"Don't do that. Don't end your life. Living has got to be better than death." Voice said nothing. "I don't know shit about you, Voice, but I do know you're making a difference. No one ever said that to me when I was on the job. Now, look at me. I'm a soon-to-be mom. A wife and I have more money than I could ever spend."

"Tangible things have never meant shit to

me, Agent. But it was nice of you to think we're the same." Her laughter this time sounded sad. Like she'd already given up on her life. "Avery's family will be coming in on the next flight from Paris. They didn't come from there, but that's how they were routed. And trust me when I tell you that they will tell you less about their lives than I have about mine. Avery will be in on a military plane, then a domestic that lands at the Columbus airport three days from now. Pick him up or not, but he'll get to his family himself if necessary."

"I'll be there." Writing down the information, what little there was, she asked Voice how she would know when he got to the airport. She said his wife would contact her. "All right. What else can I do for you?"

"For me? Nothing. I need nothing from you or anyone else right now." Harris wanted to stomp her foot and tell her to give her what she wanted. When she spoke again, Harris stiffened in her chair. "Hang on."

The wait seemed to be an eternity. But when she spoke again, Harris was standing up and ready to go to her. If only she'd allow it. The pain she heard in her voice, the noises that she could now hear, made Harris know that something else was going down.

"I don't have an address." Harris told her she'd find her if she needed it. "I'm shot to fuck here, Harris. It's an ambush coming to the Columbus airport. I can only think they know that Avery is coming in." She heard cursing and had to smile. She did it in several languages too. "His family is safe. They'll be at the hotel I'll name in a minute. Go and get them. Guard them with your life or so help me, I'll hunt you down and make it look like you fell into a chipper feeder."

Shivering at the way she'd die — there was no doubt that Voice would indeed do what she said — Harris vowed that she'd protect them. When the line was suddenly cut off, her phone indicated that there was a message. Not only did it have the longitude and latitude to the hotel, but also the street address. When she started to put the phone down, having just the title of unknown on it, she received pictures of the entire family coming in. When it beeped the third time, it said *safe or die*.

Calling for backup, she was shouting orders to everyone she came across. Even Shep, who had been in the backyard, came running when she yelled for him. Time, she knew for some reason, was running out for Voice.

On the road in less than twenty minutes felt like it was too long. Harris still didn't know where Voice was or how she was supposed to get to her.

Less than an hour later, they were pulling into the hotel drive. Leaving the car, she knew her men were all over the place. She counted three of them in the lobby as soon as she came through the door.

The gun to her head had her pausing and putting her hands up. "I'm Agent Marshall. I've come to get the Avery family." The gun pressed harder into her head. "I have a text message from the woman that sent me. She said there was a showdown at the airport, and I needed to get you out of here."

"Show me your library card." Confused, Harris reached for her wallet and then her card. "Hold it up where I can see the number on it." After what seemed like an eternity, she was told that she passed. Asking about the library card, the person who she turned to look at laughed. "No one thinks about the shit they have on them at all times that might give them away to someone. And no one thinks about a little thing like I asked you for when I was to use it to ID you. See? Smart cookie, Voice is."

The young man who was standing there with his gun at his thigh just stared at her. Harris didn't know him. However, she was sure that if asked, he'd be able to tell her anything about herself. Asking the kid how old he was, he grinned at her again.

"Seventeen. You're lucky I was the one that drew the short straw. If Mom had come out here for you, you'd have been knocked around more. She's not good with strangers." Harris asked if all his family could handle a gun like he did. "Yes. Or we'd all be dead."

Just like that, "We'd all be dead if we didn't know what the hell we were doing." As Harris was being dragged to the elevator, he said nothing. Apparently, he'd been told not to make small talk. She knew for a fact that it would give you away every time. Once inside the room, she looked at the people there.

"You must be James Avery." He put out his hand but didn't speak. She looked at the woman standing next to him. "Intel on you says that you have four children. A wife as well as a couple of dogs."

"I have three children, no dogs. My middle child you've met—Jamie. The oldest is Beth—she goes to places like this as my wife. My youngest child is in the bathroom with a gun loaded and pointed to where you're standing right now. We don't fuck around." Harris said she could see that. "My wife was killed five years ago when someone figured out who I was. Anyone in my family gets hurt, and I'll do to you what I did to him. My family is all I have in the world."

"I believe you." She started to turn away and looked back. There was something there, a click of something that she needed to think about. "Holy fucking Christ. Voice, she's related to you. Sister, I'm betting."

Before anyone could tell her yes or know, she felt the sting of something in her arm and turned toward the girl and watched her as she faded in and out. They'd given her something. Something to knock her on her ass. At least she hoped so.

"It'll not hurt your child. But I can't have you going around spouting off shit that you have no right to. Just relax, Agent Harris, and have your husband Shep take my kids to your house. I'll come and get them soon. I have to find Paige." Nodding, she reached out to Shep to tell him she needed him. "He'll not be able to come through the door, I'm afraid. Also, you should know that we're jags as well. My sister changed us all when she was changed. Just rest. You'll be fine in a few hours."

She hated it, more than she would ever admit

to. But there was little to nothing she could do now that she was lying on the bed. Harris let it take her under. The sooner she got this out of her system, the sooner she could kick someone's ass. Mother fuck, she hated being treated like this.

Chapter 9

Rodney didn't care for the way this person presented themself. He was interviewing someone to take over the school nurse spot, and so far, he'd only found one person that fit the bill. But he didn't like her. Didn't care one bit for her. Rodney thought if they had to work together, they should at least be able to tolerate the other person. He wanted to stab her in the eye with a fork.

"Look, buddy. You need someone to come in and put bandages on the little tyke's knees, and I'm the perfect person for that. I have a good education, a good constitution, as well as years and years of experience that come with doing a job for so long. Just sign off on the paperwork, and we'll both be happy." But he wasn't. Not even a little bit. Rodney glanced at Rebel. He wished now he'd kept his mouth shut when he'd told her he wanted to do the interviews. "What is the hold up here anyway? You have some special way of looking into my life. I've already told you I don't have any skeletons in my closet. I'm an open book."

"My wife is going to conduct her part of the interview process." The woman, Brenda Smyth—'With a y,' she told them every time she said her name—actually rolled her eyes at him. "She's going to finish up for me. I have a call to make."

"Coward." Winking at Rebel, he wasn't a foot from her when he heard Mrs. Smyth talking. "Shut up, if you please. I'm conducting this interview, not you. Now, where is it you last worked? And don't just tell me it's no longer in business. I want a name and someone to contact."

"This is going to take all day." Rebel told her it would take as long as it took. "Oh, for the love of Pete. I'm here. I have a license to be here. Just give me the job, and we'll both be happy. You're wasting my time here, and I don't care for it."

"Well, la-de-da. I don't care if it takes me three more hours. I'm going to hire someone that fits the bill. The only bill you're fitting so far is annoying the shit out of me. Now, tell me the name of the last place you worked." Smyth said she was leaving.

"Don't let the door hit you where the sun don't shine on your way out. I think I said that right. Your grandda told me that one. Next?"

"I'm still sitting here. I'm not leaving until you understand that I'm going to get this job."

With a snap of Rebel's fingers, Mrs. Smyth simply disappeared. Rodney didn't know where she was, but out of the room was just fine with him. Then he heard her pounding on the doors, telling them to let her back in. Rodney told the staff there today that they were to call the police if she got any more abusively verbal to them. It was a nice Saturday today, and Smyth should be enjoying it more than pounding on the door.

The next three people didn't have any nursing skills at all. He had put in the ad that they would need a minimum of three years' experience, but no one seemed to be reading that. They were turning more away because of that than they were getting any work done. When the next person sat down, she handed over her resume and smiled at them. He fed the information to Harris so she could do a check on the woman.

Got it. Also, I have house guests as of last night. Don't say anything to anyone. He said he'd never do that. *I know you won't, but I'm pissy and aggravated that they got the drop on me. I would like for you to come and meet them just so I can get them to trust me. They don't, in the event, you're wondering. They're only here because their aunt is someplace hurt, and I was a last option. I don't want to be last in anything, just so you know.*

She gave him the rundown that she found on the nurse in front of them. "I'd hire her as a nanny. But there is one blot on her record. How do you suppose she knew how to contact me?" Rodney was confused for a moment and told Harris that. "The Voice. Paige. How did she get my phone number? It's not like I'm listed. The woman there, she has an ex-husband. I don't know how their relationship is. Ask her."

He did as he was told, still trying to figure out what Harris was going on about. It had been three days, and she was still asking them questions about the woman. After getting the information from Wanda, Rodney waited for Harris to get back to him.

This went on for another twenty minutes. Finally, he had enough and told Harris to shit or get off the pot. They were trying to run a business here. Even after he realized he'd pissed her off, Rodney didn't care. She'd been beating this dog to death, and they needed to move on.

You're right. I'm sorry. Don't think I'm going to let you speak to me like this often, but you are right when I bitch about something when you need me. He thanked her. *I'm sorry, Rodney. I truly am.*

She was keeping up a steady stream of information to him after that. They needed to hire three people, and so far, it looked as if Wanda was going to be one of them. Also, the woman that had come with her, for security reasons, she told him, Caroline Jamison, was going to fit the bill.

It didn't take them long to finish up the interviews after that. Harris said she was sorry a few more times, but they were on track to getting done, and he was happy with that. Even Rebel told him not to worry about Harris. If she gave him any shit, she'd take care of her.

The women in his family were very powerful. Scary powerful. His own mate was a grand witch, and she scared the shit out of him on a daily basis. And she wasn't able to hurt him. As he was packing up his things and taking Rebel's too, he felt a sudden wash of fear roll over him.

"Someone that we know is in trouble." He asked Rebel if she knew who it was. "Nope. I'm not even sure if it's trouble, pain, or just that we know them. This is some weird assed shit if you ask me."

"I agree." Then when she stiffened again, he waited for whatever was going to happen. "What is it, Rebel? Do we need to take off?"

"I do. Not you." He asked her why not him. "She's not terribly trusting. I'm going because she is a little bit of a witch and needs me."

"All right. I guess."

Then she was gone. Getting into his car, he wondered if he'd get used to this happening. People bouncing in and out of his life. The magic would wake him from a sound sleep. It was always important, but so was his rest. Going home, he wondered what he'd get himself into tonight. Nothing that he'd had planned, that's for sure.

He ate his dinner in the kitchen, watching television with their cook. After he was finished, he went to the living room to take a nap. He loved the fact that there wasn't a television in this room. Rodney could do whatever he wanted, nap or read, and there were no distractions. Hell, he could—

"What is it?" Rebel appeared in the room with him, and she had a man over her shoulder. Taking him from her, she disappeared again, this time returning with a woman over her shoulder. Taking them up to the bedrooms, he put the man on the bed and began undressing him to see where all the blood had come from.

"Where am I?" He didn't get a chance to answer the man before he started telling him he couldn't tell anyone he was there. Not even his family. "The woman that came for us, did she get my sister too?"

"Yes. I didn't see much of her, but she's in the other room." The man closed his eyes, only to open them a few seconds later. "Where are you hurt?"

"I'm shot, but I just need to shift. I'm all right. Go to my sister, she's not all right. Nor can she shift right now. It'll weaken her more." Nodding, he asked the man if he could do anything for him now. "No. I'm just desperately wanting Paige fixed up. Go on, I'll be all right. I swear to you."

After checking the wound that had indeed been a through and through, Rodney went to the other room to help Rebel. The woman in there would not be able to shift her wounds away. Nor would she live long if she even tried to shift into whatever she was. It occurred to Rodney that he had no idea what the man was either. Helping Rebel, he told her what he'd found out about the man.

"Which is very little. How about you?" Rebel told him where she'd gone and how she'd found the two of them. "You just entered a warzone and got them both here? Christ, that's amazing. I'm proud of you."

"Don't be. I have a feeling that if either of these two dies, we're going to be on a long list of shit jobs for the rest of our days." Rodney asked her if she knew who the woman or man was. "Nope. I mean, other than a name, nothing. She's Paige, and he's James. All I heard about them as I boogied out of there with him. When I returned for her, I had to break her out of a jail cell that looked like something you'd see in zoos. Where you'd want to keep the animals that misbehaved a great deal."

They worked on Paige for nearly three hours. Setting up an IV was the hardest part. Nothing would penetrate her flesh very well. Finally, they had to resort to using a very large needle to make the mark, then stab it into her that way. The two of them put nearly four hundred stitches in her body alone. Her legs and arms were a different matter altogether.

As they were finishing up, James came into the room looking as fresh as a daisy. "I hope you don't get too upset with me. I put a couple of scratches in your flooring. I'll pay for its repair." Rodney told him not to worry about it. "How is she doing? I've never seen her down before. In all the years we've worked together, I've never seen her wounded or even hurt with a broken nail. This is scary for me."

"Are you related to the people at my brother-in-law's house?" He told Rebel he was their father. "They're good and well trained. I have to admit that to you. When I went there to talk to Harris about something, I was down on the floor and spread out before I even knew there was anyone else in the house."

"Good to hear. Just because they're on domestic soil doesn't mean they should be lax. I'll have to tell them what you said." She nodded. "Is she going to make it?"

"Yes. For the simple reason that she's an immortal. However, you weren't when I got there to get you." He said he didn't think it was in the cards for him to live forever. Then he looked at her sharply, asking her what she meant by her statement, "The vampire there when I arrived, the person that was with you two watching over you, they gave you enough blood that put you over the edge of immortality."

"Fucking bastard." James said he was sorry for cursing. Rebel told him it was a second language for her. The three of them laughed. "He said he'd watch over us until you came. I don't know how he contacted you, but I'm—"

"He didn't. Your sister did." He asked her what she meant. "She's part witch. I don't know how strong—all I can feel from her now is pain. But her being injured this badly called out to me. Had you not been there with her when I arrived, I would have left you for dead. But she told me you were to come here first. I did what she wanted."

"I don't understand." Rebel told James she didn't either. That she was a grand witch and that the two of them must be important to someone higher than her. "I don't know who it would be. I mean, there are any number of people watching out for us, but as for her calling to you, I don't know."

"We'll get answers when she's ready to give them. For now, we'll keep it quiet that you're here with her." James nodded. Then he sat down in the chair by the bed and held his sister's hand. "Your family, won't they miss you?"

"No. They know that when I want them to know where I am, I'll tell them. As for now, we have to assume that someone knows she's hurt and I am with her. The fewer people knowing that, the better." He looked at the two of them. "I'm sorry I can't give you more information. But it is literally a matter of national security that we aren't found or killed."

"I can live with that. I can use a little magic to keep anyone from coming into this room. There is staff that you might hear. Also, and this is a biggy, if I tell you to move your ass or anything else that will keep me and mine safe, you'd better fucking know that I'll hurt you badly if you don't. Deal?" He laughed and told Rebel he understood. "Good. Then we should get along just fine and dandy."

Rodney didn't know what was going on. But so long as everyone was working well together, he was fine with that. But all bets were off if anyone came here with the thought of hurting his family. That would include the kids at Harris's home. He had an entire shadow that he'd bring around if anything happened to anyone.

Before You Go...

HELP AN AUTHOR

write a review

THANK YOU!

Share your voice and help guide other readers to these wonderful books. Even if it's only a line or two, your reviews help readers discover the author's books so they can continue creating stories that you'll love. Log in to your favorite retailer and leave a review. Thank you.

AWARD WINNING, BESTSELLING AUTHOR

Kathi Barton, a winner of the Pinnacle Book Achievement award as well as a best-selling author on Amazon and All Romance books, lives in Nashport, Ohio, with her husband, Paul. When not creating new worlds and romance, Kathi and her husband enjoy camping and going to auctions. She can also be seen at county fairs with her husband, who is an artist and potter.

Her muse, a cross between Jimmy Stewart and Hugh Jackman, brings her stories to life for her readers in a way that has them coming back time and again for more. Her favorite genre is paranormal romance, with a great deal of spice. You can visit Kathi online and drop her an email if you'd like. She loves hearing from her fans. aaronskiss@gmail.com.

Follow Kathi on her blog: http://kathisbartonauthor.blogspot.com/